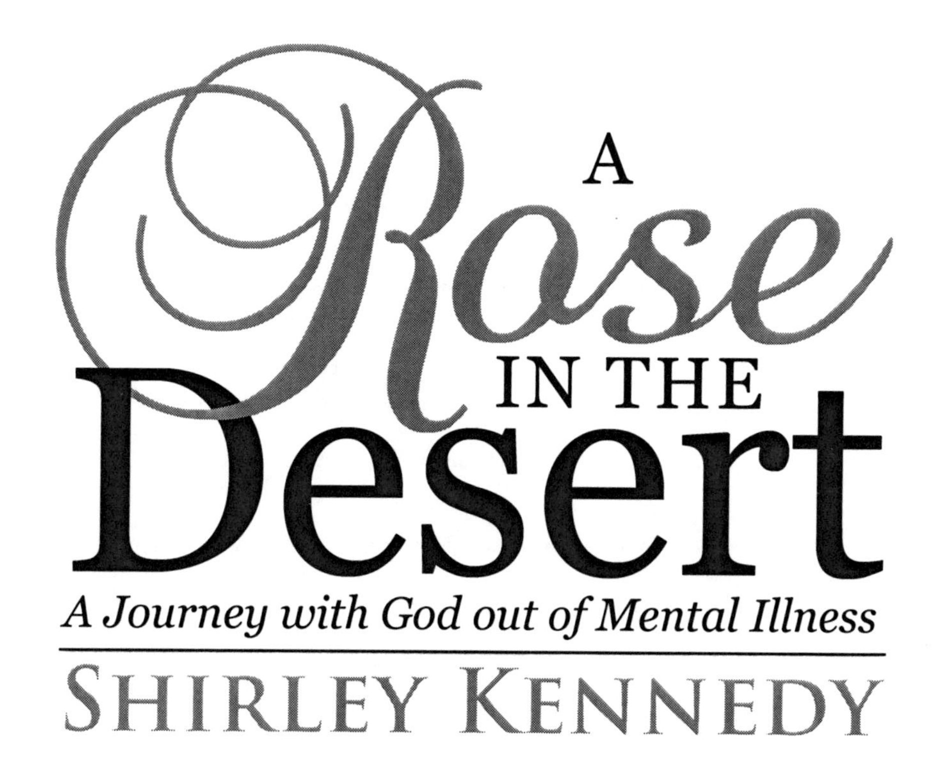
A
Rose
IN THE
Desert
A Journey with God out of Mental Illness
SHIRLEY KENNEDY

WESTBOW
PRESS
A DIVISION OF THOMAS NELSON
& ZONDERVAN

*This book is a work of fiction based on a true story. Unless otherwise noted, the author and the publisher make no explicit guarantees as to the accuracy of the information contained in this book and in some cases, names of people and places have been altered to protect their privacy.*



WestBow Press books may be ordered through booksellers or by contacting:

WestBow Press
A Division of Thomas Nelson & Zondervan
1663 Liberty Drive
Bloomington, IN 47403
www.westbowpress.com
1 (866) 928-1240



ISBN: 978-1-5127-3320-4 (sc)

Library of Congress Control Number: 2016903592

Print information available on the last page.

WestBow Press rev. date: 03/31/2016

# Contents

# *Foreword*

When I first met Shirley a number of years ago I never would have guessed that she had a story like this to tell. A life-loving woman, open and passionate, Shirley gives no outward indication that she has ever suffered from a mental illness. Laughing while she talks, her life now displays an abiding peace. When adversity comes, she chooses life rather than allowing herself to fall into a dark pit.

To reach this point, however, Shirley has faced painful truths. In her early twenties, her whole life in front of her, the doctor's diagnosis of manic depression (now known as bi-polar disorder) is not easy to hear. After the darkness of her first manic episode, she is eager to move on and is surprised when another episode strikes her. As she hits bottom through a deteriorating marriage, separation, and divorce, accompanied by intensifying manic episodes, she continues to cry out for help to the only One she knows loves her. She asks for and receives Counsel. She finds herself again and again in the pit, but Hope finds her. She follows with courage, determined to pursue health.

As I read her story I ached for her; I was amazed at the 'coincidences' in her life: somehow she always seemed to find what she needed when she needed it. Parts of her story resonated with my own life and struggle; I needed to hear how she came through it all. Dare I believe

I can find wholeness too? Although still a part of who Shirley is, her former pain has become a deep well of compassion – an anticipation that the telling of her story will give hope to others to embrace a similar path of healing.

Lynda Warner
Journalist

# *Acknowledgement*

My children Paul, Susan, Samantha and David played a very significant role in my journey towards mental health. My love for them kept me from suicide more than once. I would not allow myself to leave them with the shame and guilt of such a decision no matter how tempting at times. The details of their smallest accomplishments brought a joy that encouraged my heart and as we celebrated together, I drew strength acknowledging that any amount of emotional pain was worth it for moments like these.

I also want to acknowledge my friend Lynda Warner who persevered with me throughout two writings of 'A Rose in the Desert'. In addition to teaching me literary skills, she challenged my thinking and expression of thoughts to benefit my reader. At times, she asked me tough questions and caused me to see the details of my storytelling in a different way. I appreciate all these things about her, but mostly the steadfast friendship she offered me throughout the journey.

Shirley Kennedy

# 1

## *The Diagnosis*

"Mrs. Samson, come in and have a seat," said Dr. Bernier, the psychiatrist. "I regret to say that you are manic depressive, which means you have a chemical imbalance in your brain. You will be subject to episodes like the one you just went through for the rest of your life. It will be difficult to hold a job as the episodes will continue to disrupt your life. Unfortunately, there is little understanding or acceptance of mental illness in our society."

He took a deep breath before he continued. "It will get worse as you age. The episodes are triggered by stress, but you are unlikely to know when they are about to happen. Comparatively speaking, your case is very severe, judging by this first episode. Your risk for multiple episodes in one year will increase if you have any children and as you go through menopause."

He pointed to some medication. "The treatment for manic depression is lithium carbonate – a mood-altering drug. It helps minimize the extreme highs and lows, but does not necessarily eliminate the occurrence of the episodes. Lithium taken over a long period of time may destroy one of your kidneys. The good news is that you have two of them. I recommend that you start treatment immediately. If you do not take the medication you may stabilize, but it will take a substantially longer time. Any questions?"

'What............!' Shirley's thoughts rolled around in her head. Her eyes darted about the room. His death sentence repeated itself again and again in her mind. Her mouth opened, but no words came out. She was in shock.

"Mrs. Samson. Do you have any questions?"

"No, no," she said, lips quivering.

"Think about what I said and let me know if you decide to take the medication. If you think of any questions, don't hesitate to ask."

At the age of twenty-seven under the threat of losing her adopted baby, abandoned by her husband and the fear of facing life alone without family or friends nearby, Shirley suffered a total break with reality and landed in the hospital. She thought it was a one-time occurrence, so she ignored the diagnosis and medication until she was forced to think about it again.

Shirley was not aware of the emotional instability in her life until her early twenties. When her boyfriend of four years decided to date other women in their university years, she felt penetrating rejection and anger. Stretches of depression started slipping in, but she told no one how she was feeling. She overslept, resulting in missed classes and became so paranoid at times that she might follow her impulses to jump off the twelfth floor apartment that she would not go anywhere near the balcony door. She would not even sit at the end of the table closest to the door. Shirley cried often and emotionally she felt like she was falling apart. She called her childhood grandfatherly friend and told him what was happening. He came immediately and took her to his quaint little home facing Lake Ontario. They talked for seven days. He asked her every question he could think of to understand her emotional state of mind. He affirmed her and spoke comforting words to her. When he thought she was more stable and able to cope with her university situation, he brought her back to Hamilton with the request that she keep in touch often. She agreed and did so, going on to finish her second year of studies.

Her boyfriend Tom had a change of heart that summer and wanted to date again. Shirley jumped at the chance and they saw each other often. One evening they were strolling along one of their favorite places to walk. "I want to get married now, not two years from now," she declared.

"But we can't. I have two more years to finish my degree and I promised my brother that I would travel with him before I started working," he replied.

"I want to be married **now**," Shirley repeated. "I want to be first in your life, not third or fourth."

He pulled her into himself and kissed her on the forehead. "We will be married. Just be patient," he said.

Mid-July they went canoeing and she told him her plan. "I love you, Tom. I have decided not to go back to university this fall unless we are married. No, hear me," she said as he was about to interject. "They have living quarters for married students and I could get a job while you go to school. I am not going through another two years like these past two years." she said. "If we don't get married, I will go to my sister's in Germany. I want to be married **now**," she declared.

"Shirley, Shirley, Shirley! What am I going to do with you? You aren't being reasonable. Married living quarters are expensive and you know my parents would never agree. Nor would your dad," he replied.

"I don't care what our parents think. We're over twenty and we could just go and get married. My sister and her husband were married when they were seventeen and nineteen. Tom, please …… please," she said. Tom did not respond. After thirty minutes they packed up and paddled back to the camp in silence.

Their relationship was strained for the remainder of the summer as they realized they would be going their separate ways come September. Finally, the day came and he took her to the airport. They cried as they held each other, but there seemed no way to close the gap. Her tears flowed for some time during the flight. She felt like the kid who wanted to play on the team and shouted, "Pick me. Pick me." But he didn't.

She met Pete a few days after she arrived in the small town where her sister lived in Germany. He offered to take her out and show her the area. He wined and dined her and she fell in love with all the attention paid her.

His proposal of marriage after eight weeks came at the same time as a letter from Tom asking her to come home and marry him. Her heart knew she wanted to marry Tom, but she was so afraid that when she returned home, she would be met with more waiting and disappointment. She was tormented for days. Pete was with her. He made her feel like a princess and so did his friends. She wanted to live in that fairytale land and forget all the pain inside.

Shirley accepted Pete's proposal and wrote a goodbye letter to Tom. Having made her decision, she ignored any warning bells with Pete. He made it very clear, "I don't want any children. Are you okay with that?" She felt stunned. She couldn't believe he really meant what he said. She was sure she could convince him to change his mind. She said, "Oh, yes," hiding her confusion and desire for children in their marriage. She focused on becoming the new bride and took in all the attention that went with it.

From the beginning of their marriage, Shirley felt like Pete's sister rather than his wife. Intimacy between them did not grow. She knew it was important to a lasting relationship, but she didn't know how to help it develop.

Pete stayed late in the evenings with his co-workers while she read books from morning to night. Depression returned. She regularly walked the streets of the little German village they lived in and spoke aloud the anger that was inside. "I'm trapped! I should have gone back home and married Tom. He's the only one I'll ever love!" she cried. Her thoughts turned to God. "And my mother! I was so foolish to believe that you, God, would heal her! Instead, you let her die! No one else in my family believed you, except me. You betrayed me! I hate you, God. I trusted you and you failed me. You probably aren't real anyway. You're some kind of a psychological need - not a real God," she shouted. The rain covered her tears; the heaviness of her depression remained invisible.

Shirley wanted to talk to her sister, but was so ashamed of her failing relationship with Pete that she said nothing. She made herself believe things would change between Pete and herself. Then they were posted to an isolated base in Labrador, Newfoundland and she felt like she stepped into another fairy-tale land. It was a much more social place and she embraced the uniqueness of the experience. She attached herself to every activity that made her feel good.

Shirley also co-taught a pre-kindergarten class at the American school and one day the words of a little child stopped her dead in her tracks. "Mrs. Samson, Mrs. Samson! Guess what I 'm doing tonight!"

She bent over to look at her face to face. "What, Mary Ruth? What are you doing tonight?"

"I'm giving my heart to the Lord Jesus," she said in her sweet, southern accent.

Her mother also bent down to look into Shirley's eyes. "We'd love you to come if you're able. Mary Ruth would be truly blessed."

"I…I…I'd… love to, but I have a meeting I have to attend," she stammered. She turned to another child and started talking to her to avoid further discussion with Mary Ruth or her mother.

At home she was constantly talking to Pete about having children. Their friends were pressuring him too. Adoption in Newfoundland was quicker than having a child naturally. Pete finally agreed to adopt. He knew how much she wanted children. Shirley boarded a plane for Gander, Newfoundland four months after their application was accepted, to pick up their baby. He was a dark, eight-week old infant smothered in oil. He had brown eyes just like Shirley's and would quickly become the apple of her eye.

Pete and Shirley had no idea how to be parents and so for a short time, they grew closer through the challenge of parenthood. They delighted in all the changes and stages in the first year and gave him all their attention. They were almost disappointed when he had to go to bed. Paul was the enjoyment of all their childless friends as well.

Six months after Paul arrived, they were posted to Vancouver Island, B.C. This was the coveted posting. The sandy beaches bared themselves for long stretches in the summer and a new ski resort had recently opened only forty-five minutes away. The scenery was majestic in all directions. It rained frequently like Germany, but after all the snow and sub-zero temperatures in Labrador, Shirley was ready for a change.

Shirley observed that something was wrong with Pete from the very beginning of their relocation. He started to withdraw from her. Each night he played with the baby briefly, but meaningful communication with her disappeared. Night after night, he crawled into bed, put his back to her and turned out the light.

One night, she pried into his silence. "Is anything wrong at work?"

He didn't roll over to face her. "No, no, everything's fine," he replied.

"Are you mad at me?" she asked.

His back answered her question. "No, no, I'm just tired. Everything's fine."

Finally, the bomb dropped. Pete came home one night and said, "We have to talk." Her mind raced to another woman, a terrible disease, but she could never have guessed what he was about to say. "I should never have married you. I didn't want to even on the day we got married. I was tempted just to get in my car and drive to Switzerland. I should have," he said as he paced back and forth, his head looking downward. "I've been living a lie all this time and I'm not going to live like this anymore."

She was stunned. After several moments of deadening silence, she got up and went to the bedroom. Her head was swirling. "I've never heard of anything like this before," she said to herself. "This can't be happening; this can't be happening to me. I've never done anything to deserve this. The past seven years have all been a lie! How could he do this to me?" She grabbed her long hair and pulled hard until it hurt. "He's ruined my life. How could he lie to me all these years? I will never be able to face my family. He's a coward. A low down coward! Two-faced liar!" Then the realization. "My baby, my baby! I'm going to lose my baby too," she thought and slumped onto the floor, sobbing.

Still crying, Shirley returned to the living room. "Do you realize that if we separate now, we could lose our son? We've only been in BC for six months and the adoption agency requires that Paul be in a stable home for 12 months before the final adoption takes place."

"I know, Shirley. I can't make promises right now. I'm at the end of my rope. I just wanted to tell you what is going on."

Pete slept on the couch that night and many nights following. Communications remained minimal between Pete and Shirley except when they interacted with their son, Paul. Shirley took the baby to her sister's home in Ontario for a few months while Pete tried to sort out his thoughts with a counselor. After many weeks of separation, they decided to stay together until the adoption was finalized and then they would decide what to do.

Shirley had no friends on Vancouver Island - no one she could talk to. There was no family anywhere near. If an opportunity to talk to someone ever arose, she had to be careful not to speak of their predicament for fear of losing Paul. The anger inside of her was growing into rage. She was incensed with the unjust situation! She hated feeling powerless and trapped. She cursed her husband under her breath every day.

Shirley watched the papers for any activities she might do in the evening for a diversion. She saw an ad for a Christian speaker. It gave her the warm fuzzies of her youthful church days, so she decided to attend. She soaked up all the wonderful stories of how much Jesus loved her. Then he told her she was a sinner in need of a savior. *"What…………….?"* the voice inside her head screamed. *"I am not a sinner! I am a good person. Pete is a sinner! If that guy says that sinner thing one more time, I'm out of here!"* He did and she left.

In the four months of waiting for the final papers, they socialized little with others and even less with each other. Their time was focused on their son and whatever activity they could find to distract themselves from the pressure. One night when Pete was out, Shirley watched Jesus Christ Superstar on television. Again the warm fuzzies came as she experienced the familiar names and situations. She began to think about God again.

*"Don't touch that!"* Shirley screamed at her baby. She smacked him and then when he cried, she dissolved in tears. She erupted like a raging volcano more frequently with every passing week. She muffled her screams in the pillow for fear that someone would discover what was going on in their home. The thought of losing her baby caused extreme emotional pain. Shame at her failing marriage washed over her in waves. She lost her appetite. Eventually her sleep was affected, leaving her very anxious. She had thoughts of putting Paul in the car and taking off, but she didn't know anyone in British Columbia. She had nowhere to go.

One evening while she was alone and lying on her bed, she felt like she was going to lose her mind as she started thinking about her mother who had died ten years earlier. Intense mourning rose within her and she screamed to no one in particular, "I want to talk to my mother!!" Her spirit rose up and she looked down at her body on the bed. She started to move through outer space. She passed through the stars, moving out into the universe. The further out in space she traveled, the more afraid she became. "Stop, stop! Bring me back!" Suddenly, all of her was back lying on her bed. She had no understanding of what had happened. But she felt heard by someone in the supernatural realm and she was afraid to pursue it any further.

The next night she had the same sensation that her head was exploding. "God, if you are real, I need you to show up," she screamed. When she threw her legs over the side of the bed in the morning she heard,

> *The Lord is my shepherd; I shall not want.*
> *He makes me to lie down in green pastures;*
> *He leads me beside the still waters. He restores my soul;*
> *He leads me in the paths of righteousness for His name's sake.*

*Yea, though I walk through the valley of the shadow of death,*
*I will fear no evil;*
*For you are with me;*
*Your rod and Your staff, they comfort me.*
*You prepare a table before me in the presence of my enemies;*
*You anoint my head with oil;*
*My cup runs over.*
*Surely goodness and mercy shall follow me all the days of my life;*
*And I will dwell in the house of the Lord forever. Psalm 23*

Shirley did not see Jesus. She did not see an angel. She heard the words, although she did not know where they came from. But she believed God was real and she had hope. For the moment, she didn't feel alone.

She wanted to find out where those words were from. She borrowed her neighbor's bible the next day. She was flipping through the pages when she realized the name of Jesus was everywhere. She started reading page after page. "Oh no!" she concluded, "I must be Jesus Christ!" Her mind interpreted the words of scripture so that if Jesus said something and she had experienced it, she concluded that she must be Jesus. Except for the brief encounter she had with God in hearing what she would later discover was Psalm 23, the frazzled thoughts of her mind were pulling her away from reality.

The following night, she had strong thoughts of revenge, obsessing about her desire to hurt Pete as much as she was hurting. She fell asleep out of pure exhaustion and awoke abruptly in the middle of the night. Her heart was racing and she was in a cold sweat. The words 'born again' heard numerous times from various television programs were ever present in her mind. She had an overwhelming urge to get the butcher knife from the kitchen, stab Pete and Paul so they could become born again and end this nightmare they were living in. She started towards the kitchen, her heart pounding, when from somewhere in her head she heard, *"Run! ... Run!"* She turned towards the front door and ran outside onto the road barefoot and in her nightie. Pete heard her go out the front door and he stuck his head out the window.

"Shirley, come back in here! You'll make a spectacle of yourself," he yelled.

"No, I'm not coming in! Not until you get that guy Donny over here."

"It's 2:30 in the morning. I can't call him now."

"I don't care what time it is. Call him or I'm not coming in."

He disappeared from the window and she randomly started ringing neighbors' doorbells in the hope of getting into a warm place. No one answered. *"These people are imaginary! No one lives in these homes!"* she concluded. *"I wonder if there would be anyone at the hospital. It's too far to go to discover that there's no one there too. I must be insane!"*

"Shirley, Shirley, Shirley, Shirley. Come back to the house!"

She slowly walked back. "He'll be here in about 15 minutes. Come inside."

"No! I'm not coming into the house with you," she said for fear that the overwhelming compulsion would return.

"Have it your way." He tossed a coat and a pair of shoes out the door.

Her neighbor's Pastor Donny arrived shortly afterwards. He helped her put her coat and shoes on and led her into the house. He spoke briefly with Pete and then asked him, "Is this what you want for your wife?"

"No," Pete answered.

"Then let me take her to the hospital."

"Okay."

He did just that.

The attendant from emergency put her on a stretcher and rolled her down to the psychiatric ward. Her body was involuntarily bouncing all over the bed. The doctor started injecting her with some drug. She smacked his hand in order to prevent him.

"Don't do that," the doctor said. "You need this in order to settle down." He motioned for four other people to come and assist him in holding her down while he continued the procedure.

Shirley awoke on a May morning in the spring of 1977, in the psychiatric ward of the local hospital fully drugged. Her movements were jerky spasms and she drooled from what felt like a permanently opened mouth.

"Medications!" a nurse bellowed from behind the desk. She watched as a herd of people came from every direction, lined up in front of the desk, and silently waited their turn to receive medication. She had no desire to be given any further drugs. She hoped the nurse would miss her in her round-up.

Shirley made her way over to the couch of the common room and stood in the warmth of the blazing sunrays. "Well, God, I don't know what has happened these past few days, but I don't ever want to go back there again. Please teach me how to get out of this mess and I'll follow you wherever you want me to go."

Three days later, the psychiatrist's words pounded into her head. "Well, Mrs. Samson, come in and have a seat. I regret to say that you are manic depressive, which means you have a chemical imbalance in your brain ... You will be subject to episodes like this for the rest of your life..."

Shirley left the doctor's office and found a quiet place where she could talk out loud to God. "God, I don't believe him. I refuse to accept his hopeless report. I really don't understand all that he just said, but it doesn't add up." She looked upward and asked with the simplicity of a child, "How could You be so real that morning and there be no hope? I know you are real. No one can take that away from me. I don't know if this is a one-time thing or something I'm going to have to deal with all my life." She sat in silence a few minutes and then she added, "Give me the courage to walk after you and understand your plan for a healthy mind."

# 2

## *Heart of a Young Girl*

She was christened Shirley and called Shur, Shurl and at times Sherman – like the tank. Her father thought it was a strong name. He so desperately wanted a boy he was willing to wager one week's pay that she was that son and clung to his bet as if to will the baby to be a boy. Her mother endeavored to do all she could to make her look like a little girl. She dressed her in frilly little dresses and took a long time each day preparing her hair so that it would fall in perfect blonde ringlets. One day when Shirley was around four with her dolly in hand, she was sitting quietly on the back stairs that led to the kitchen when she heard her dad come through the back door of the shed to the kitchen.

"Mike, have you noticed anything different in little Shirley's behavior this week?"

"Oh, Michelle, you know I don't notice stuff like that. She looks fine to me."

"Mom was just saying she looked a little withdrawn and forlorn for our Shirley. She said she just wasn't herself."

"That woman is always coming up with these things, I swear. She can see things no one else can see. And that don't mean that it's real."

Shirley got up from the stairs and quietly made her way to her favorite place in the attic. "It's okay, dolly. I already told them what happened. They didn't believe me when I told them about that bad man who gave me yucky kisses and hurt me. I won't try to tell them again." She arranged her dollies in a semi-circle and lifted her pencil to lead them in song. "Okay, now…"

As a child, Shirley was fascinated with God. Sister Pauline, her grade one teacher, taught the children about Jesus and a few other people from the Bible using a huge, colorful flip chart. Sister Pauline's love for God was obvious and she played all the characters in the story with great enthusiasm.

Although it meant getting up at 6:45 a.m., as a young girl Shirley loved going to Mass, then having breakfast at her Grandma's before leaving for school. Sometimes her Grandma was also at early Mass and that was the best. They would talk and laugh all the way down the hill to her house. They had breakfast together and Shirley would leave for school.

Shirley often returned to her Grandma's house after school and sometimes she stayed for supper. After they cleared the table, they went to her bedroom to say the rosary. Her grandma led and she responded. Shirley tried to slow the speed down because she wanted to think about what they were saying, but as soon as it went back to Grandma, the pace picked up again. And when they were finished praying, it was time to play cribbage. When her Grandma won, her whistling would get louder and longer. She always made Shirley laugh.

Sister Pauline taught the children that Jesus was real. She made it sound like He had a voice and He would listen. Shirley decided to take her questions to Him directly.

"You are going to do what?" her friend Susan asked her. "If you get caught in that sanctuary, you will get into such big trouble. You have to be a priest or an altar boy to go in there when there isn't a Mass going on. Why do you want to do this anyway?"

"I am looking for some answers and I believe we should be able to talk to God and hear His voice."

"You are such a dreamer. You always come out with weird ideas. You should forget the whole thing. I've got to get home." And she left.

Shirley was nine when she decided to follow through with her idea. She slipped into the sanctuary and positioned herself close to the tabernacle. This was the Holy of Holies – the gold box that held the unused, blessed wafers that were transformed into the very body of Christ. She swung her legs back and forth off the pew, hoping to get up a bit of courage.

Shirley had been taught not to talk in the sanctuary and she was finding it a bit more difficult than she thought breaking the rule. "Hi, God. I just wanted to talk to You for a few minutes. I know You are very powerful because you healed those people in the Bible and You did those miracles with the fish and everything. I just wondered if You could talk to me. I mean I would like to hear Your voice." After ten minutes of silence and her heart pounding much faster than normal, she said, "Okay, God. I know you are a busy person. I will come back another time." She never got up the courage to return and try again.

Between her father and her two older teenage sisters, their home was one yelling match after the other. Whenever a fight broke out, Shirley ran for the closet. She would shake and cry and wince with every additional loud sound and bang. She told her mother that she wanted her to lock Shirley up in the attic when she became a teenager.

When she was twelve Shirley became very ill with a great deal of pain in her stomach and delirious with high fevers. Her family had been vacationing in the United States and quickly returned to get medical help in Canada. She awoke in a bed in the hallway of the hospital in her hometown. There was a little girl, younger than herself, pushing an IV pole coming towards her. She stopped beside Shirley's face. "Hi, my name is Sally. I get to go home in two more sleeps," she said happily. She put her face down and came up with a sad face. "My grandma says that you're dying. Are you dying?" she asked. The nurse turned towards the little girl and shushed her away. Looking to Shirley, the nurse said, "Don't you pay any attention to her. She has no idea what she's talking about."

But the idea stuck. It made sense to Shirley. She had no strength. She felt like she was dying. Shirley asked her mother for a rosary on her next visit. Then she overheard the doctor whispering to her parents at the doorway. "I wish I had more news to give you. We've run every test we know to run. She continues to weaken and we don't know why."

Shirley was glad to have her rosary. She felt like she could talk to God again. "God, everything I know about heaven sounds boring. Does it really mean that I get to sit on some kind of merry-go-round and watch the earth below? I don't get it. Maybe there is more to the story I don't know. You comfort my grandma when she is sad. Please make me better or take me to a fun place," she finished. She thumbed the crucifix and made the sign of the cross. "In the name of the Father and the Son and the Holy Spirit, Amen." Still holding the crucifix, she began "I believe in one God the Father Almighty, Maker of heaven and earth…" Her thumb slipped to the first large bead. "Our Father who art in heaven, hallowed be Thy name…" And then to the first small bead, "Hail Mary full of grace, the Lord is with thee…" And then her favorite, "Glory be to the Father, and to the Son and to the Holy Spirit. As it was in the beginning, is now, and ever shall be, world without end. Amen." Then on through the five sets of Our Fathers, Hail Mary's and Glory be to the Fathers to complete the rosary just the way she did it with her grandma.

The following morning the doctor came in. He took her arm and lifted it up. "Open your eyes wide," he instructed her. Then he used his fingers to open them really wide. "I thought so," he said and left the room quickly.

It was hours before her parents came that morning. "Hi, Sweetheart, how are you doing?" her mom asked.

"I'm okay."

"The doctors say you have hepatitis. Until your skin turned yellow, they weren't sure. Now they can treat you and you should be able to go home in another week."

"That would be great, Mom."

She stroked Shirley's forehead. "You're going to feel tired for quite some time, but at least you'll be able to sleep in your own bed."

"Yeah," she said as she silently thanked God.

At home again it didn't take long before the fighting started.

"Your curfew was 11:00 o'clock," yelled her dad.

"I was only 10 minutes late. I tried to get here on time. I did my best. I can never please you!" her oldest sister yelled back. Shirley heard her dad hit her sister. Then she would hear her mom scream, "No, Mike, no!" Shirley hated the sound of yelling and screaming. In moments like this, she wanted to get out of the house and run away.

Physical abuse lessened as she grew older, but the verbal abuse and false accusations continued to wound Shirley. She had watched her two older sisters break the rules regularly. She thought she could learn from their mistakes. She was sure that if she did exactly what her father said, she would escape his wrath. She was wrong. She came to the same conclusion her sisters had. Her dad would never trust her.

In the middle of sorting out her life with her dad came the most devastating news of her life. In February 1965 the doctor opened her mother's breast to examine a lump and concluded that it was benign. In June, her mom went back to the doctor because there was a problem with her breast. It was cancer. Surgery was scheduled for September. Michelle went for a mastectomy and the removal of lymph nodes under her arm, but the cancer cells continued to multiply daily and she had a hysterectomy two weeks later. Michelle went for chemo and radiation therapy at a hospital in Toronto.

"Shirley, Sally, come here. I'm down in the kitchen," Mike called. They thought they were in trouble and slipped into the chairs quietly. Their dad was leaning against the counter with his hands in his face. "Your mom," he said and began to cry. The girls glanced at each other, their eyes rolling. "The doctor says your mother has less than two years to live," he continued. Mike was still crying. Shirley looked at her sister. Sally lowered her head. Shirley felt numb and could not grasp what he had said. She went to her room and stared at the ceiling, unable to cry.

The next day she told her friends as they walked to school. "Oh, Shirley, that's a lie. You are always telling stories. I saw your mother two days ago and she looked fine. She can't be dying. You just made that up didn't you?" asked Susan.

"No, really. I'm not lying! I'm telling the truth!" Shirley shouted and walked away. She didn't speak to them for several days and she told no one else.

Shirley spent every free hour playing basketball or other available sport. High school classes finished at 4:00 p.m. and she went straight to the gym. If there wasn't a game, there could be a practice, but if nothing was scheduled, she practiced drills for volleyball, basketball or track. She walked the one and a half miles home by herself in rain, sleet or snow because it felt better than taking the bus and having to talk to someone. She often fell asleep at the table. She studied in her spares and went back to the gym as soon as school was over. She believed as long as she kept busy, she wouldn't have to think about the reality of her father's words.

One afternoon while playing against the top rival team, Shirley was leading the charge down the court when she was distracted by something that seemed familiar in the balcony above her. She wouldn't allow herself to look up until she was on the bench. She surveyed the students and families above. She spotted her dad! He had never been to a game before. She felt happy, afraid, and shocked. She couldn't let his appearance interfere with her performance, so she blocked him out. As often happened, she was high scorer again for her team that day.

"Dad, you have never come to my games before, so why today?" she asked as they drove home.

"Your mom thought it was a good idea. Besides I knew you were a chip off the old block. I wanted to see for myself."

That night at the supper table her excitement spilled out. "You should've seen me, Mom. I faked this really tall girl to the right and then to the left and went right in there and scored on her. It was great!"

"Yes, if there's one thing you're good at, Shirley, it's faking," her dad said.

His words felt like icy water being poured over her on a winter's day. Each time she risked revealing her heart, she heard words spoken to her that caused her to shrink back inside herself where she was silent yet safe.

After Shirley's mom went for chemo and radiation therapy, her body began to change. Her cheeks were puffy and her eyes looked tired all the time. She started taking more naps and she had no energy.

In January 1967, Michelle had the opportunity to watch her two grandchildren play in front of her as she lay on the couch. Her one daughter had flown in from Germany with her little girl and her other daughter from Peterborough was at the house with her daughter daily. In the following months their mom began to fade away. She had medication for the pain, but often it was not enough. She was either in her bed upstairs or lying on the couch downstairs.

Shirley prayed. "I know you are the God Almighty. I know you parted the Red Sea. I know you healed people when You were here on earth. I know You heal people today. My God, my God, please heal my mother. Take my dad. He's the bad one, but please don't take my mother. She's the only one who really knows me and still loves me. I will do anything you ask of me. I'll even become a nun. Anything, God. I'll do anything. I know this is a small thing for You and it will mean everything to me. Please hear my cry!"

Shirley's mom continued to get worse. She was in bed all the time. Shirley's uncle, whom she seldom saw, dropped by. He was whispering with her dad. "What's going on?" Shirley asked anxiously.

"We're bringing your mom's bed down to the living room so she can see what's going on. It will be easier on her and you gals and your grandma. You won't have to be going up and down the stairs so often," her uncle said.

"Can I help?"

"You can bring us the sheets after we bring your mom down," her dad said.

Her uncle and Dad supported Mom's frail body as she struggled down the stairs and into a chair. Shirley grabbed the sheets and they tore the bed apart and reassembled it in the living room.

Michelle was moaning in the chair. Grandma came from the kitchen with water and medication. Soon they had her settled in her new location. "Thanks, Mike and Gary. That feels so much better," Michelle said.

Too frequently Shirley's eyes caught a glimpse of a mother she no longer recognized. The puffiness in her skin made her look fat. Her sleep talking was to someone in her childhood and there were times when her mother was awake that she did not know who Shirley was.

Shirley sat on the front stairs, looking through the railing at her mom lying on the bed. The warmth of the sun from the front door was shining on her face. "My God, my God. Heal her. Please heal her. Bring her back to life. I know you can heal her. Please, God, don't let her die. I trust you. Please give her a miracle." Shirley believed God would heal her.

Her uncle came to visit her the following week. "Mom, she can't go on like this anymore. She isn't getting enough pain medication. She needs to go to the hospital where they can take care of her."

"Okay, we'll talk it over with Mike when he comes home from work."

"Mom, he's not thinking straight. He's too weighed down with all the decisions." He picked up the telephone, dialed and said, "Yes, I need an ambulance to 6024 Frank St. Her name is Michelle Stevenson. Yes. Okay, thank you."

He leaned over his sister's bed to tell her the plan. Her eyes fluttered and it took all her strength to say, "Thanks, Gary." And as she breathed in deeply, "Deanne?"

"She's on her way. She should be leaving Germany by the end of the week. I'll make sure she goes straight to the hospital as soon as she arrives. You just rest until the ambulance gets here. I'll get a hold of Mike at work and let him know what's happening." He stroked her head affectionately.

It wasn't long before they were loading Shirley's mom into the ambulance. The lights were flashing, but there were no sirens. People were gathered on the sidewalk across the street to watch the unusual event. Grandma and Sally and Shirley went back into the house. "Grandma," Sally asked, "Is Mom really dying?" Grandma did not respond.

Shirley turned and walked toward the front stairs so they couldn't see her fighting tears. She went up to her room and through clenched teeth proclaimed, "My mom is not going to die. She is not going to die! God will heal her!"

A few days later, Shirley was at school when she got word that her dad had collapsed at work and he was in the hospital too. One of the teachers took her straight there and she went to her father's room. She needed to find out if her dad was dying too. Her grandma wasn't there and her dad was asleep. A nurse came up behind Shirley and put her hands on her shoulders. "Are you his daughter?"

"Yes."

"He'll be fine, Dear. He's just exhausted and with plenty of rest, he'll be back to normal."

"Okay, thanks."

Shirley went upstairs to her mother's room. Her mom looked very peaceful. No one was there. "God, I don't understand what you're doing. Why are you waiting so long to bring Mom her miracle? Surely, you won't let her die! Please let her live! You've raised people from the dead. Please, God, let her live."

"Hi, Shirley," Grandma said as she entered the room. "Did you see your dad?"

"Yes."

“Deanne will be here tomorrow if your mom wakes and asks for her.” Grandma tenderly stroked her daughter’s hand, put her head down in resignation, and then left the room.

“Please, God, heal her,” Shirley cried out again.

Shirley’s sister did arrive the next day from Germany. Shirley didn’t know how life and death worked, but her mom died later that day. Deanne had a brief time to say goodbye and her mom was gone. Shirley remembered very few details of that day. She didn’t remember talking with any members of her family. She didn’t even remember who came and told her that mom had died. She entered a world of numbness and the events of the following days passed by her as though they belonged to someone else.

It felt shameful to watch her dad break down so many times in public. She distanced herself from his all-consuming grief and chose instead the numbness of her control. God was far, far off. She felt cold and icy towards everyone around and when someone said, “I know how you feel,” she wanted to shout, *“No, no you don’t!”*

The wake at the funeral parlor went on for two days. She spoke words to people who came, but they were not connected to her heart. She was alone in the black chasm of her mind and moved robotically until it was time to close the casket.

On May 8, 1967 Shirley lost her mother and she gave up on her God. Her mom had been her protector, her safe place, and the only one who knew her and loved her. Her God had betrayed her. She vowed she would never trust Him again.

# 3

## *A New Family*

"No, I'm not going to take the medication," Shirley said.

"Do you understand the implications of that choice?" the psychiatrist asked her.

"I'm not going to have another breakdown. I got sick this time because I was under too much pressure," she said.

"Well, that's true, but your first episode was very severe, which indicates that there are likely to be more. The medication is there to help you, not hurt you," the doctor said.

"I am normal and I don't want to take medication that will alter me in any way," she insisted.

"I can't force you. If you change your mind, come back and see me," he said. She left his office with the hope she would never see him again.

Shirley wanted to distance herself from this horrendous first episode and get on with a regular life. She landed a position at a nursery school which was one of four centers of the regional daycare society. Because of her ability to keep accurate records, she was asked to be the Business Administrator for the society before the year was out. For the first time she was beginning to feel like she was getting on with her life. She knew she wanted to be married again and Paul needed a father, but her confidence in her ability to choose a good partner had been shattered. "Father, I need your help. I need your choice for a husband and father. I hate the idea of dating. Please bring only Your choice to me. Lead and guide me with your word. I trust you to speak to me."

Shirley wasn't sure if she was ready, but when her girlfriend insisted that she come for supper to meet someone along with her boyfriend, she gave in under pressure. She hadn't been on her own for very long and she felt very shaky about even being introduced to a man. The conversation was awkward as the four of them were from very different backgrounds. Allen was a miner and had recently been in an accident, which accounted for his crutches. Their conversation was mostly about the mining industry and Shirley had little to say. She wanted to recoil, get out of the conversation, and get out of the room. Allen feasted his eyes on her, but she had mixed feelings as to how she felt about all the attention she got that night.

Two nights later there was a knock at her door. There stood Allen. He had hopped on one foot from his truck to bring a frozen sockeye salmon to her. "Best fish you'll ever eat," he said. "Mind you, it's even better fresh, but this is all I have now." He gave her the cooking instructions and by then he was all hopped out. She thanked him as he used the last bit of strength to hop back to his truck.

Shirley unwrapped the fish and put it in the sink to thaw. "Ooh!" she said. "The head is still on," *God, who is this guy? How old would he be? That is obviously a beer belly he totes around – and if I understand the meaning of a redneck – he's a redneck! Surely this is not the man you have for me,*" she thought.

He called later in the week to see how Shirley and Paul liked the fish.

"Yeah, it was quite nice," she lied.

"You said the other night that you went to church. Where do you go?" he asked.

"The one on Main and 5th Street," she answered.

"Would you mind if I joined you sometime?" he asked.

"Yeah, I suppose," she said, but she wasn't really sure.

"I started thinking about the Big Guy again after what happened in the accident. I was lucky I only got a broken leg out of it," he said.

"Did you used to go to church?" she asked.

"Yep. We had to go to a little gospel hall in Mayford Creek every Sunday. I didn't always listen, but I was there," he said.

That was the beginning of their relationship – church at least once on Sunday and sometimes twice. She was so impressed with a man who acknowledged his need of God that her heart began to soften towards him.

By the time they had dated a year, Allen was back to work and there was an offer on her house. Pete was pressuring her to sell as he was still paying the mortgage. She took the first offer, signed the papers and found herself with a month to move. She panicked, feeling completely unprotected making her own decisions. She called several places to rent and the rent seemed too high for her income.

Shirley felt more like a little girl than a grown woman with a child. She needed her father to help her make good decisions, but she was too proud to ask. She was still hiding from the shame of her mental illness episode and was reluctant to ask for help from anyone in the church or anywhere else she might be questioned about the details of her life. She didn't want to look like she didn't know what she was doing. When Allen returned home that weekend, she begged him to let Paul and her rent a room from him. She wanted someone to take care of her. She didn't care if his current roommate had to leave. She didn't care what it looked like moving in with a man she wasn't married to. She needed to feel safe and protected. Shirley recognized that the intensity of her insecurity was not logical. She was being driven by a force she did not understand and there was an urgency to fill the gaping hole.

Allen and Shirley began to take their relationship more seriously as the months went by and the word 'marriage' slowly surfaced in their thinking. Allen took Shirley and Paul to meet his family in Mayford Creek. She fell in love with his parents, especially his dad. She discovered his mom was a Christian and had prayed for a Christian woman to marry her son. Shirley knew his mother didn't like the idea that she was in the process of getting a divorce, but she alluded to the fact that life wasn't always ideal. They had a wonderful visit and when they returned to Vancouver Island, Shirley started making arrangements for the three of them to visit her family in Ontario.

The visit was disastrous for Shirley. She felt like a totally different man showed up to meet her family. His redneck ideas surfaced in every conversation and she was embarrassed, losing hope that her family would ever approve of him. What she didn't see at the time was that she was a totally different woman in front of her family. She needed to show them everything was perfect in her life and when Allen wasn't perfect, she suffered great discomfort in the situation. All she wanted to do was get back to Vancouver Island and get out of the relationship. Their conversation during the trip home was strained on her part and she looked forward to time alone.

Finally, she cried out to God. "Father, it was so awful. I was so embarrassed in front of my family. Why do I think I love him?

Is it because he takes care of me? Is that enough for a life-long commitment? Shouldn't I feel more love for him instead of contempt when he doesn't do what I think he should do? Lord, I would do anything for You. I would even marry this man I am so unsure of. But I must know that you are asking me to do this and not me steering things in the wrong direction. Surely somewhere in this Bible there are words about a bride and bridegroom and marriage. If this is your will, please take me to these words. I will do what you ask because you are a good God and you give good gifts. I will trust you and obey," she said.

Two days passed and her eyes fell on the passage from Isaiah 62:2-5: *You shall be called by a new name, which the mouth of the Lord will name. You shall also be a crown of glory in the hand of the Lord, and a royal diadem in the hand of your God. You shall no longer be termed 'Forsaken', nor shall your land any more be termed 'Desolate'; but you shall be called 'Hephzibah', and your land 'Beulah' (married); for the Lord delights in you and your land shall be married.... And as the bridegroom rejoices over the bride, so shall your God rejoice over you.*

Shirley wept and wept. When she saw the words 'forsaken' and 'desolate,' she was deeply aware that God knew all that was in her heart about herself. For no matter what picture she projected to others, her identity was wrapped up in forsaken and desolate. The idea that she could delight the Lord was a new concept. It brought a flood of hope for a more intimate relationship with her God.

And then she cried because she believed her God was asking her to marry Allen, which involved a greater degree of trust in God than she ever knew. She was so disappointed. She had thought this was the opportunity to break free from this relationship and find someone who would be more like her lost love, Tom. This was the last time she would question God about His will for her relationship with Allen. Shirley stood firm in her belief that the Lord had asked her to marry in trust. Her prayer remained the same, "I will do what you ask of me." They were married in the United Church in 1979.

Shirley believed in the years that followed, Allen and she missed the goodness God had planned for them. They were like the Israelites who missed the shorter journey of less than two weeks to the Promised Land and instead took forty years living in the desert.

About six weeks after they were married, Shirley lay wide-awake one night while Allen lay snoring beside her. Shirley felt a pain-like sensation in her fallopian tube. She began to think about the article she had read recently, how some women could feel the egg drop from the ovary into the fallopian tube. And since there were sperm present – Praise God – she knew they had just conceived. In the midst of the bursting joy, she believed she heard the Lord tell her that Allen and she would have a son. His name was to be David and he would be a blessing to his parents and to the Lord Himself. Her heart was pounding and she shook Allen until he was awake. "I believe God said we are going to have a son and we are to call him David," she said.

"That's nice, Dear," he said and rolled over, going back to sleep.

*God, why doesn't he get You? A miracle takes place - a very personal miracle - and his response is 'That's nice, Dear'! I hope he gets to know you the way I do soon. O God, you are such an awesome God! I want to spend the rest of my life telling people about you.*

Very shortly, it was confirmed that Shirley was pregnant. She told both friends and acquaintances that God told her she was going to have a son named David.

"What if it's a girl?" one friend challenged her.

"It's a boy. He told me so."

"What will you do if isn't a boy?" she asked more softly.

"If God said it's a boy named David, then that's what it is," and Shirley dismissed any further ideas about the subject.

In that same month, she became pregnant with an idea after praying with a friend. "Liz, I believe the Holy Spirit instructed me to start a Christian nursery school."

"Well, you certainly have the background," she answered. "And the Lord could show you how to take care of the details. I'll support you and pray."

After six months of obtaining the necessary paperwork, the application was done. Shirley had asked the Lord what He wanted to name the nursery school. Repeatedly, she saw the words "Little Children" in the chapters of 1 John. "I write to you little children…1 John 2:12. Little children, it is the last hour… 1 John 2:18. Beloved, now we are the children of God… 1 John 3:2. She named it Little Children's Christian Nursery School. Then she looked for a supervisor or manager and a location in which to hold it.

In January of 1980, she received a call from her pastor who knew about the project and her need. "I just had a lady in my office who has been a supervisor in nursery schools for years. She has moved up to this area from Victoria and when I told her about your project, she was excited and wanted to know more. You may want to talk to her."

"Thanks, Pastor Donny," Shirley said and took the number.

Margaret Fyfe was the most gracious, gentle, grandmotherly woman Shirley had ever met. When Shirley told her the details of how she had started, Margaret rejoiced with her and was ready to be on board. The two of them and others continued to pray for a location.

Shirley's former employers, the regional daycare society, rented space from the church Margaret and Shirley attended, the United Church. Each time Shirley prayed about the location on her own, she came up with same answer: the United Church. But it didn't make any sense. The daycare had been there for years and she knew the church would not ask them to leave. So they continued to pray and search for a location.

In late May of that year, Pastor Donny called her, "I have some good news for you. The daycare society has given notice that they no longer need the church building after June 30th. They thanked us for the use of the space for all these years, but they have found another location."

"Thank you, Jesus!" Shirley shouted. "God is so good! Have you told Margaret?"

"I think you should tell her," he said.

"Thanks, I would love to. I'll also call the ladies that have been praying with us. What an answer to prayer!" In September 1980 Margaret Fyfe welcomed the first child to Little Children's Christian Nursery School. Within months the school was filled to capacity. Eventually, two of Shirley's own children would attend.

From a high of answered prayer, later that same day Shirley arrived home to a low she could not fathom. As she approached the front door, she could hear Allen yelling. In the living room, Paul was on the floor with Allen over him, kicking him, screaming at something Paul had done. Then Allen smacked him on the head. In an equally loud voice, Shirley started yelling, "No! No! No!" Shirley leaned over to pull Paul away and she could hear Allen quiet down behind her as she left the room with Paul. Later they spoke about it, Allen justifying his own behavior as he told her what Paul had done. But somehow, while she was in the same room with Allen, she could think of nothing to say. She could not form words to express her horror. She didn't know if she was angry or afraid. She just felt numb; she wanted what she had clearly witnessed to go away.

After she put Paul to bed that night, she went to her quiet place in the house. *"God, I don't get it. I've known Allen for two years and he's never once lost his temper and hit Paul. Now I'm married to him, carrying his child and this happens. Did I miss something? Is life just about suffering? This is like when I was a little child. Useless, uncalled for behavior. Please make it go away."* She had memorized a scripture earlier that day. Some of the words were floating around in her head and she decided to look them up to get it right. *"I have been crucified with Christ; it is no longer I who live, but Christ lives in me; and the life which I now live in the flesh I live by faith in the Son of God, who loved me and gave Himself for me."* Galatians 2:20

Shirley lowered her head and said to the Lord, "*God that really doesn't sound good to me. It sounds like suffering even when I know I am right. You told me in the beginning that I would need to trust you with everything, and although I don't understand it, I will trust you. Hold me tight because I find this scary. I love you, Lord; I will obey."* She was comforted by blind obedience to God at this time in her journey of faith because it meant she didn't have to make decisions nor take responsibility for them. Suffering was what Shirley knew and she would not encounter the love of the Father for some years to come.

From the beginning of their marriage, Shirley and Allen had prayed together at her request before they went to bed. However, Allen's willingness to do so dwindled as time went on. He was very uncomfortable talking about his feelings and reluctant to share any inner thoughts with his wife. They were negotiating life on the surface and there were only rare moments of intimacy where their hearts were unveiled to each other. She could not predict the explosive anger fits. She was simply thankful for the times in between incidents and dealt with the eruptions as best she could, not realizing the effect on her own mental health and on Paul. They started counseling early in their marriage, but nothing changed. Shirley felt trapped, but did not know what to do about it.

Allen was extremely excited about their pregnancy and took great pride with each pound Shirley gained. He attended all the prenatal classes even when it meant supper in the vehicle after he had raced home from the north part of the island. It was a hopeful stage for Shirley and there were few eruptions.

At last it was time for their baby to come, along with the many hours of discomfort, pressure, and pain that accompany birth. Allen arrived at the hospital in the early evening. Seeing her panting and breathing as they had done in class, he commented, "You're doing great, Dear." He went to the far side of the room and struck up a conversation with a nurse about mining. If Shirley hadn't believed she was under some obligation to act kindly toward him as his wife, she would have thrown some large object at him. His focus was always on work and she wanted this time to be an exception. She was afraid to express her anger with him under normal circumstances and this did not look like the best scenario to create a scene.

Exhausted, Shirley spent much of the time walking up and down the hallways trying to get some relief from the pain. Around 11:00 p.m., she walked back into the room to see Allen settling into a bed the nurse had provided for him. "Shirley, I'm really tired. Wake me up if anything happens."

Shirley was so angry with him that she couldn't speak. Alone! Again! She went for yet another walk in the hall to try and sort out her emotions. *Jesus, I feel so rejected. Why can't he love me the way I need to be loved? He made this baby too. Why does he get to sleep while I experience the pain?* Through her timed breathing she heard

Him say, *"My Little One, I will not in any degree leave you helpless or relax my hold on you."* Hebrews 13:5 Jesus' comfort brought her much needed tears of relief.

After 12 hours of hard labor at 11:23 a.m. the next morning, Shirley heard the baby cry and the doctor's voice. "You have a beautiful baby girl, Mrs. Peterson. The nurse will clean her up and bring her to you. You are going to need a few stitches, so I'll get started."

The nurse brought their baby in a blanket exposing only her head. She had a slight tinge of red hair contrasted with her bright white skin. Allen snuggled in alongside them. He wanted to hold the baby before she tried to nurse her. As tears of joy rolled down her face, she looked at their baby in his arms and thought, *"You are so beautiful! I don't understand why you aren't David, but you are the most beautiful baby I've ever seen."*

Alone in her room, confusion overwhelmed Shirley again. *"I don't understand, Lord. You said it was going to be a boy and his name would be David. What happened? Where is David?"*

*"My Little One, Allen cried out to Me for a daughter even before you met him. Your daughter is a gift to him. She will be the apple of his eye. You will have a son named David in My time. Trust Me with all your heart."*

Because Shirley had insisted that her child was a boy, she had not considered a girl's name. As she thought of what to call her, she thought of her best friend growing up. Susan. It felt like a strong name to her. Allen agreed to the name, though he seldom used it in her early years. To him she was Booby-bear.

*"Susan, Lord. That's a good name for this beautiful little girl."*

One evening shortly after Susan's birth, Paul and Shirley were watching an episode of the Incredible Hulk. It was Paul's favorite show, but each time the man transformed into the Hulk, Paul would bury his head into her lap. "What is the matter, Honey?" she asked him.

He responded with, "He's too scary, Mommy."

"It is okay, Honey. I'll protect you."

As the words left her mouth, she realized that she could not always protect him from Allen's scary outbursts. Shirley buried her head in the sand once again, hoping it would all go away. She wanted so much for the two of them to have a healthy, happy relationship, but she did not know the way. Then she heard a noise coming from the hallway. She used it to distract Paul from his fear. "What's that sound?" she asked him. "Is that Daddy singing to the baby again?" She took Paul and led him by the hand down the hallway to Susan's room. There stood Allen leaning over the side of the crib, Susan's hand grasping his baby finger, singing his finest country and western song to his little girl. Paul and Shirley giggled softly to each other, turned, and went back to their show. She wondered if Allen would ever have that same tender kind of relationship with Paul. Life seemed secure and peaceful for the moment and Paul was glad to have one on one time with his mom, but he was caught in her delusion that life would be better tomorrow.

# 4

## *Second Episode*

On the day Shirley took Susan for her six-month check-up, she drove straight home as she knew Susan needed a nap. Shirley was taking the baby out of the car, when she heard a loud voice coming from the house. She ran with Susan in her arms and burst in the front door to hear Allen yell at Paul, "You stupid, little jerk! I told you never to touch that!"

Paul was on the floor crying. Shirley bent over to try to soothe him.

"I've told him over and over again not to touch my gear!" Allen screamed.

Shirley took Paul by the arm and carried Susan to her room to prepare her for her nap. After Susan settled, she took Paul to his room. "I'm sorry Daddy hurt you. I will talk to him tonight. We'll get this thing straightened out. Paul, you are not a bad boy. You need to listen to your dad when he tells you not to touch his stuff." She took him into her arms. "I love you so much."

In Shirley's mind she practiced what she wanted to say to Allen when they were alone. *Allen, you can't talk to a little child like that. You'll crush his spirit, his confidence, and his idea of how a father is supposed to act towards his son. He looks up to you. He needs you. I don't object to discipline where you would send him to his room or take away privileges, but words can leave bruises as well as your fists. We said we wanted a family. Let's work together to create the kind of family we want.*

When the moment finally came, Shirley approached Allen as he sat on the couch reading the paper. "Allen, I want to talk to you."

"I don't want to talk to you," he replied as he got up and prepared to go to bed.

All of Shirley's courage vanished. The two of them finished the day in silence, their hearts brewing with unresolved anger.

In contrast to moments like this, were the many fun family times where they visited extended family in Vancouver, spent the day at Stanley Park, visited Allen's parents at Mayford Creek or were at the rink watching Paul play hockey. It seemed that about every six months there would be another incident involving Allen and Paul. In between, Shirley lulled herself into a false sense of security, believing that it would never happen again. She didn't know how to deal with the reality she was facing and she lived in denial. Her decision would adversely affect her mental health and create great confusion in Paul's heart.

For Susan's first Christmas, the family went back to Ontario to visit Shirley's entire family. Everyone was able to be there and the teenaged cousins had a lot of fun fussing over the baby and Paul. Shirley was on edge that Allen might do or say something that would cause her family's disapproval. On a frosty morning a few days after Christmas, Allen was bored and decided to go for walk. When he returned he was visibly happy and excited. "I just bought a truck! They phoned the bank back home and my account manager approved it. It's a super cab. It has lots of room for the kids. You'll really like it! It's thousands of dollars cheaper than out west," he said.

"And just how do you propose to get it out west?" Shirley's oldest sister Diane asked.

Shirley felt embarrassed with Allen's announcement and her sister's in your face response.

"That's easy! Shirley and the kids can fly and I will drive the truck back. It should take me about three days," he said with great satisfaction.

"Does this thing have wings?" Diane asked.

"Oh, I think three days should be enough. I'll sleep in the truck for a few hours along the way and then I'll have a day to rest up before I go back to work."

Shirley was so angry with him that she left the room. He hadn't asked her about the truck and now she had no choice but to take two children on a nine-and-a-half hour trip from Toronto to Vancouver Island all by herself.

As she climbed the stairs, she heard Diane's voice question him. "Did it ever occur to you to talk to your wife about such a major purchase?"

"Oh, I make lots of money. My account manager would never approve it if it was questionable," he said.

Shirley's sister had raised the questions she was thinking. She was furious that Allen never answered the question and she had no hope her words would be heard even if she voiced them. She was embarrassed in front of her family about their inability to communicate; she said nothing.

After a six hour flight, a forty-five minute retrieval of their vehicle, another forty-five minute drive to the ferry terminal, a ninety minute ferry crossing and an hour drive up the Vancouver Island with a five year old and an eight month old, Shirley was exhausted, frazzled and stressed out. She put the children to bed and dissolved into tears. She spoke out loud to Jesus briefly, "I am so angry with that man. I hate him. I hate him," she cried as she crawled into bed. She said nothing to Allen of how she felt when he returned with his truck.

Susan had turned one and Paul was in grade two when Paul started lighting fires. The first time Shirley found him, he was on the balcony just off the kitchen. He had taken the matches from the fireplace, lit pieces of paper, and sent them floating over the railing to the ground below. "Paul, what are you doing?" she asked alarmingly.

"These are planes that got hit by bombs. Aren't they neat?" he replied.

"Honey, you can't play with fire. It's dangerous. Now put that flame out this minute," she said. Reluctantly, he obeyed.

Two days later she was standing on the balcony again when she spotted a fire in the tall grass just beyond the boundary of their property. She secured Susan and flew down the back stairs to investigate. She found Paul with his best friend James feeding a small fire with dry grass. "What do you two think you're doing?" she yelled. They both began to stamp the fire out. She picked up the lighter and the pieces of paper from the ground. "Where did you get this lighter from?" she asked.

"It's my mom's," said James.

"I'm getting Susan and we're all going over to talk to your mom."

When she told Anna the story and gave her back the lighter, Anna grabbed James by the ear. "You little brat, I told you not to touch my lighter! Now you go to your room and stay in there until I tell you to come out!"

She turned to her and said, "I'm sorry, Shirley. I'll make sure it never happens again."

But the boys were not deterred. The next week Shirley was in the kitchen doing the dishes when she sensed that someone close to her was in danger. "Lord, are you trying to tell me something?"

Shirley looked to see Susan behind her. She was fine. Paul? She hadn't seen him in over an hour. She dried her hands, picked up Susan and ran out the door calling Paul's name. When she couldn't find him in the immediate area, she headed for James' house. She ran towards the grassy alley between James' fence and the forest. There was a red gas can on the ground and the boys were trying to strike their matches. She put the baby on the ground and ran towards them. "No! No! No, boys, No!" They looked at her and dropped their matches. Anna and she agreed that they would separate the boys until they could figure out what was happening.

Shirley's doctor recommended that she take Paul to a psychologist. Dr. Jensen suggested that lighting fires was a phase and it would pass. In the meantime, he told her it would be a good idea for Paul to have permission to light fires while being supervised. Although she followed the psychologist's suggestion, she did not agree with his premise. Deep inside she believed that her little boy was trying to communicate with her and the fires were an expression of his unspoken needs. She set herself to ask the Lord.

Ten days later while watching an informative Christian program, there was an episode dealing with sexual abuse. The man was very knowledgeable and shared all aspects, particularly how it might manifest in the behavior of a victimized child. The revelation of what had happened to Paul swept over Shirley. She went to his room to awaken him and find out.

"Hi, Sunshine. Did you have a good sleep?" she asked him.

He groaned at being awakened.

"I have something to ask you. You haven't done anything wrong, but I need some information. Can you help me?"

"Yes, Mom."

"Has anyone ever touched you in an area of your body that they shouldn't have?"

"Yes," he said and a shiver went through Shirley.

"Did the person touch you in your private parts?"

"Yes," he said as he turned his back to her.

She named a number of occupations to narrow the search of who it might be but, it wasn't until she asked him if it was a teacher that he said "yes" and began to cry.

"Which teacher was it, Honey?" she asked.

"Mr. Crumpits."

She held him in her arms and rocked him for ten minutes and then said, "Thanks for helping me. Now get dressed for school and come upstairs for breakfast." She went up to her bedroom and cried.

"Thank you, Lord, for exposing the truth."

Allen and Shirley went to see the principal. After exchanging pleasantries, she told Mr. Pearson verbatim the conversation she had with Paul and he put his face in his hands.

"This is very serious business," he said.

"I agree," she responded.

Allen fidgeted, hitting one hand into another, but he said nothing.

"What made you ask those questions" asked Mr. Pearson.

"Paul has been lighting fires for some time and I believed there was something more to it. I was watching this program on sexual abuse and his behavior started to make sense. I followed the guidelines the program suggested for asking a victimized child."

Mr. Pearson was very apologetic and promised he would get to the bottom of it.

He called two days later. "Mrs. Peterson, I wanted to update you. We've had other boys reporting victimization by Mr. Crumpits. He has been released from his position as teacher. The only thing left is to decide whether or not you want to press charges."

Pressing charges meant putting Paul on the stand. Shirley vacillated between that and keeping him removed from the process. Allen wanted her to lay charges. In the end, she did not. For Paul, the fires stopped after there was some initial counseling, but the negative impact of that experience plagued him for many years.

Triggered by the inability to protect Paul, Shirley's mental illness would surface again in that same year and send their family on another destructive descent. As usual it began with a high that was greater than any drug-induced high known at that time. Shirley had every plate out of the cupboard and every decorative dish on the table.

"Mom, why are you so happy?" Paul asked.

"Because it feels so great when you know it's time to go to heaven," she replied.

"Are we going to heaven today?" he asked.

"Yes, today is the day," she answered.

"Who are all those plates for?" he asked again.

"We're going to have the wedding feast of the King. And you, child, you can just go out in the highways and byways and invite anyone you want to."

Paul scrunched up his face in disbelief at what she was saying. He was leaving the kitchen area when he tripped over Susan's walker with her in it.

"Watch out for your sister!" Shirley screamed angrily at him. He turned and ran out the front door. Susan was crying and she picked her up and shook her roughly, causing her to cry all the more.

Paul returned about fifteen minutes later. He had been crying and was accompanied by a neighbor who was a nurse.

"What's happening, Shirley?" Elena asked. "Is everything alright?"

"Everything is absolute......ly wonderful," she replied.

"Is the baby in her crib?" she asked.

"Yes, ma'am."

Elena went to the baby's room and then returned to the kitchen. She noticed some money sticking out of Shirley's bible. She opened it to see ten one hundred dollar bills. "What is this?" she gasped.

"Oh that. Well, I can't take it to heaven, so I thought I would give it away," she replied.

"Yes, Paul said you were going to heaven today. What's that all about?" Elena asked.

"Well, it's the truth. It's the plain truth, that's what she be!" Shirley said.

"Well, why don't we go to the hospital and have that blood test taken first?" Elena guided her.

"I don't need any blood test. Do you think they would send the results to heaven?" she replied.

"No, I mean the blood test to make sure the kids are okay. You want what's best for the children, right?" she asked.

"You know I want what's best for my children, but I don't think they need a blood test," she said.

"C'mon, Shirley. It won't take long and then you'll know for sure they're fine. I will put the children in my car and then we can go."

"Okay, but I don't like this. Are you trying to trick me?" she asked.

"No, everything will be fine," Elena said. She motioned for her to go. "C'mon, let's go."

Shirley gave in reluctantly.

As they entered the front doors of the building, four nurses moved toward Shirley.

"Mrs. Peterson, we are here to help you," said the lead nurse. Elena lifted Susan from Shirley's arms. Shirley started to resist and then let her go.

"I don't need a blood test. The children do," she said in confusion.

One of the other nurses took her by the arm and she pulled away. "Don't put your filthy hands on me," she shouted.

Shirley turned back to Elena and asked, "What's this all about?"

"Shirley, it's for the safety of the children and to get you the help you need," Elena said.

"You liar! You tricked me and I thought you were my friend," she blasted Elena.

Paul started crying, "Mommy, Mommy!" He pleaded, "Please come home soon, Mommy!"

Shirley turned to the four nurses and said, "You lay one hand on me and I'll fight you with all I've got."

"Does that mean you'll walk quietly to the psychiatric ward?" she asked.

"I will walk exactly where I please and I have no intention of going there," Shirley retorted.

The lead nurse nodded to the others and the fight was on. Each one grabbed a part of her body and started pushing her towards the ward. She yanked and pulled and pushed and swore the whole time. Eventually they wrestled her to the ground. And that's when she felt the sting of the needle in her buttocks.

Shirley awoke in a small room, lying on a mattress on the floor with no blankets. There was a space above the sink where a mirror once was. There was no furniture, no windows and no hot water. There was a two-inch mesh square on the only door in the room.

The mesh was so thick she couldn't see out. Jangling keys were the only warning that lukewarm food was coming. She knew this had to be psychiatric prison. She had heard other patients talk about it, but this was her first time. She sat on the mattress and began to cry. "My God, I feel so helpless. Why has this happened again to me? I just want to be normal. Please show me what's going on," she said as she dried her tears. She remained in the bleak room for seven days.

Once back on the ward, she went on a search and spotted a Gideon's bible on the shelf. She picked it up and it fell open to Isaiah 1:5. "Why should you be stricken again? You will revolt more and more. The whole head is sick, and the whole heart faints, from the sole of the foot even to the head, there is no soundness in it, but wounds and bruises and putrefying sores; they have not been closed or bound up, or soothed with ointment." She was shocked!

"Lord, how do you do it? You bring the answer to my prayers even when 'my whole head is sick, and my whole heart faints.' You are so amazing!" she said out loud. The idea that her wounds and bruises had not been closed or bound up rolled around in her mind. "I'm sorry Lord. I thought I was all better. I don't know how to get to that place. Will you lead me?" she asked.

Shirley saw the doctor the following Monday. "The medication they gave you when you came in was designed to bring you off that high and help stabilize you. Now you are sliding into the depressed phase. Are you ready to start the lithium?" he asked.

"Yes, I don't want to go through that again," she said.

"Good," he replied.

Shirley felt so defeated. She did not want to take the medication. She was as surprised as anyone (except the doctor) that she had had a second episode. She wanted to distance herself from the strange and embarrassing actions she exhibited when she became high. She wanted to be normal.

It was another two weeks before she went home and many weeks after that before there was any measure of normalcy. She cried many times a day. Paul would put his face next to hers and say, “Don’t cry, Mommy. It makes me feel so sad.” It motivated her to try to control her crying. When Allen found her in one of her crying sessions, she quickly covered up her tears and attended to one of the meaningless chores of the day. He had no tolerance for what she was going through and she couldn’t risk his anger in her weakened position.

The doctor explained to Shirley that the medication would eventually stabilize her moods, but that it would be necessary to determine the underlying emotional causes through professional counseling for long term mental health. Although she was not aware of it at the time, she had years of unresolved anger to address. Real and lasting healing would take time. Even as this second episode was winding down, events were stirring for the next one.

# 5

## *Another Girl*

"Yes, you are pregnant." Shirley's doctor sighed deeply. "You have yourself a bit of a dilemma. If you stay on the lithium, there is a risk of harming the baby. If you stop the lithium, you will most likely trigger an episode. The healthiest choice for you and your family is to have an abortion."

"Abortion is not an option for me," she responded. If God gave us a child, He will surely show us how to walk through this pregnancy without taking a life."

"So that would make your choice…?" the doctor asked.

"I don't want to kill my baby and I certainly don't want to risk harming the baby either. So that only leaves one option. I will stop taking the lithium."

"Based on your history, that is not the best choice for you and your family," he stated.

"I understand your position. Based on my faith, this is the best choice for me and my family," she said.

Allen was very unhappy with the possibility that Shirley might have another episode.

"What are we going to do with Susan and Paul if you get sick again?" he asked.

"I don't know, Allen. I don't know. All I can do is take care of myself the best I know how. I'll get plenty of exercise. I'll put someone in place that I can talk to so I don't get all bottled up with my emotions. I don't know what else to do! But I am not hurting or killing our baby!" She turned and walked out of the room. Once again, they were on opposite sides of the issue.

In their home the explosions of verbal and physical abuse did not happen every day, every week or sometimes even every month. They had many happy times as a family and Paul had many safe father/son experiences. Allen took Paul to hockey practice and games whenever he was at home from the mining camps. Paul was a great goalie and received praise from other parents as well as Allen.

"Did you see that save? What a great goalie!" Allen spoke of Paul to one of the other parents.

"Yeah, I'm glad he's on our team!" said Sam, Steven's father.

Moments like this beckoned her back into that false sense of security that all was well with Allen and Paul, and she convinced herself that she had blown everything out of proportion in the past.

In the third month of her pregnancy however, Shirley awoke to the familiar yelling and screaming. Allen was getting Paul ready for hockey practice. There was a problem with the skates and Allen was verbally abusing Paul. She went to the top of the basement stairs and stood watching. She was afraid. She was angry. She froze in her tracks. Eventually, Allen calmed down and said to Paul, "Get in the truck, you stupid, little jerk." Something in her died each time they went through this phase of the cycle. She wanted so much to live another way, but many times she lost hope that they would ever discover it.

Two weeks later Shirley was at the doctor's office. He recognized that she had begun to swing into the manic phase of an episode. He put her in the hospital immediately. She was placed in a private room in a regular ward and monitored.

"Has your mom arrived yet?" she asked Allen when he came to visit.

"Yes, she came over on the three o'clock ferry," he said.

"I'm so sorry I left you with such a mess."

He remained silent. She felt so guilty when he did that.

"Well, I guess I should be going," he said.

"But you just got here."

"Yeah, well……" and he turned and left.

Shirley was hurt that he wouldn't stay and angry because he didn't meet her needs. She said nothing.

During her time in the hospital, she had delusions and hallucinations. Just as quickly as she experienced them, she would return to times of being normal and wonder what all the fuss was about. At one point she was obsessed with the fact that she was carrying twins and that these boys had a destiny to save the world. "You just wait and see how important these boys are to the world," she told nurse Feldman.

"Okay, Mrs. Peterson. Maybe you ought to give those little ones a rest," she said.

"Oh, they don't need a rest," she said. "They're super human."

"Well, maybe they will be super human when they grow up, but right now they really need some rest." She helped Shirley into the bed and pulled the covers up over her.

The next morning, Shirley was flying down the hallway in a stolen wheelchair."Yahoo! Yippee!" she yelled.

One of the nurses grabbed the arm of the chair and brought her to a quick halt. "Mrs. Peterson, you can't be doing that. It's dangerous to yourself, your baby, and other people in the hallway!" she said.

"You nurses are such spoil-sports," Shirley said.

"Regardless of what we are, you need to get out of the wheelchair and walk back to your room," the nurse said sternly.

It took several more days for the symptoms of the manic phase to fade. The doctor wanted another whole symptom-free week to pass before he would allow her to go home.

"C'mon, Doctor. Please let me go home. I want to see my children," she pleaded.

"I just want to be sure that you are stable," he said.

"It's been over a week hasn't it?" she asked.

"Just one more week to be sure," the doctor commented.

A few days after she returned home, their schedule was back to normal. Paul was in the back woods killing birds with his imaginary gun and Susan was following her everywhere she went, clinging to her skirt. She was delighting in the pregnancy, wondering if this was David, but not verbalizing the thought to anyone.

That fall Susan, Paul, and she had many sessions of making bread dough men and cookies. She made the kids costumes for Halloween and they had such fun together as a family – just like everything was normal again. As they were preparing for Christmas, she noticed grandiose thoughts contending for the space in her mind and her sleep patterns were becoming very irregular. It seemed like all the fences of resistance were being torn.

She was afraid a manic phase was beginning again. She went to see the doctor.

"The baby checks out fine. How long have these thoughts been occurring?" he asked.

"It's been a few days. It happens when I wake up. It feels like I have no control over them. They feel like intruders that are forcing their way in. It's scary," she said.

"What concerns me is that your episodes come on so fast. Are you able to make arrangements for the other children if I put you in the hospital again?" he asked.

"I don't know. We'll have to do the best we can," she replied.

"I'll check to see if there's a room available and I'll give you a call as soon as possible," the doctor said.

Shirley was afraid to tell Allen. "Not again! I can't ask Mom to come over again. Can't you just handle this yourself?" he asked.

Inside she yelled, *"If I thought I could, I wouldn't have gone to the doctor. Don't you get it? I am afraid to be alone with the children and get sick! For their sakes!"* But she said nothing out loud.

"Here we go again. Our lives completely disrupted. Can't you think of anyone but yourself?" he asked.

Shirley lowered her head and began to cry with shame. She turned and ran for the bedroom. She could still hear him grumbling and complaining from the kitchen.

The phone rang in the living room and Allen yelled for her to pick it up. "Yes, doctor. Thanks for your help. I'll come in as soon as I can." Shirley packed her bag and told Allen he would have to make arrangements for the children. She grabbed the keys to their second vehicle and left for the hospital.

For three weeks Shirley contended with intense, bizarre thoughts. It seemed that once she was in a safe place, she gave them permission to come. She began telling the staff that she was going to be the first woman prime minister. It was obvious to her alone that she was the best candidate because her roots were French, English and Metis. She was a chosen child of God and she was on course for her destiny.

She talked to anyone who would listen about her greatness. To her own delight only, she danced up and down the halls singing whatever song came to mind. The staff monitored her whereabouts to ensure she would not leave.

Finally, after three weeks, the frequency of the symptoms began to weaken. She was released a few days before Christmas. She embraced the children and remembered how she had told them this would never happen again. She felt like a failure as a mother in a moment that was filled with the joy of being in the presence of her children.

The remainder of her pregnancy was quiet and peaceful. That spring she gave birth to another beautiful girl. She wanted to call her Lorraine after a cousin who looked much like her mother, but her father-in-law asked if he could name her Samantha and she conceded.

Samantha had a red birthmark that covered her nose, her forehead, across her head and down onto the back of her neck. Shirley prayed, "Father, this mark may interfere with this child's understanding of how beautiful she is in your sight and the sight of others. Please, completely remove it off her face, in Jesus name." Each time she would nurse her Shirley touched the area below her hairline and say, "Thank you, Jesus, for removing the birthmark from her face." In the months that followed, the mark on her face faded until there was no more trace of it.

It had been two weeks since she had seen Paul and Susan. It was time to retrieve the two older children from Allen's parents. Shirley was sitting in the rocking chair holding Samantha while Allen loaded the car. "Stop your moping," he said to her. "Get tough and pull yourself out of this gloom and doom nonsense. We've got to pick up the other kids from Mom and Dad's, so just snap out of it." Allen continued to carry their luggage to the truck.

Shirley was so angry with him. In the privacy of her mind, she asked, *"Where is the man who vowed 'in sickness and in health'?"* She felt numb and was losing hope that they could mend the mounting tears in their relationship. She hated being disdained by her husband.

They drove in silence to the ferry and parked on the lower deck. She lowered herself from the truck with Samantha in the snuggly and with all the strength she had, she slammed the door and started walking toward the steps of the deck above.

"What are you doing?" Allen yelled at her. She saw the two ferry workers glance towards them. She felt very bold with other people around. She walked back to the truck, opened the door and again slammed it as hard as she could. Allen moved towards her, motioning her to go upstairs. "Don't you touch me," she said through gritted teeth. She started rocking the baby up and down in her snuggly, setting her mind on how much she hated the way her husband treated her. He disappeared up the stairs.

Ten minutes later he came back downstairs for Samantha and herself. "Shirley, this is ridiculous! Get upstairs right now," he commanded.

"If you don't get out of my sight, I'm going to jump off this ferry and swim back to the island." His face reddened and he quickly went up the stairs again. The two ferry workers moved a little closer to her, feigning work. Allen came back with the captain of the ship, who gently convinced her to go upstairs and relax. He brought her to the top deck level from which he steered the ferry so that he could keep an eye on her and she would not have to encounter her husband for the duration of the trip.

They rode in silence from the ferry to his mom and dad's. The tension between them melted in the fussing over the baby and seeing Susan and Jeff. When they returned home, their lives were consumed with the care of their children, the brokenness of their relationship unresolved.

After six weeks of nursing Samantha, it was time to go back on lithium.

"You need to think about having a hysterectomy. You had two episodes of manic depression during your pregnancy with Samantha and that is very stressful on your body as well as the lives of your family," her doctor said.

"I'll think about it," she replied, but she had no intention of doing so. She had a promised child she had not seen yet. There had to be another plan of some kind. Later that day she told Allen what the doctor said.

"I agree. We can't take any more chances with you being off lithium," he said.

"Allen, I told you that the Lord told me we would have a son named David and I don't see him yet. If you really believe that it's in the best interest of this family not to have another child, you go and have a vasectomy. I have every confidence that God is able to undo that operation if I heard Him correctly. I will have a hysterectomy after David is born." And that was that. Allen had a vasectomy in the spring of 1982 by a doctor who claimed the highest incidence of success.

In the spring of 1983 Allen and Shirley got away by themselves in hopes of bringing a spark of life into their beaten down relationship. They relaxed in the soothing heat of a hot springs spa in a remote area of British Columbia and relished the quietness and excellent food.

Back in their suite, beer in his hand and wine in hers, they came very close to communicating.

"Allen, I don't understand why every five or six months there has to be a crisis, you fly off the handle, Paul takes the brunt of your anger, Susan and Samantha are traumatized, we all settle down and then the whole situation is repeated in another six months," she said. "I feel crushed and broken when that happens. I feel sad and angry at the same time."

"He sighed deeply. "Shirley, Shirley, Shirley. You are so idealistic. You think life should be perfect all the time. It is great when life goes well, but to expect it all the time – well that is not too realistic. And Paul has got it pretty good. Why, I was yelled at every day and kicked and punched at least once a week. He has got it pretty good in comparison." He paused. "Now we didn't come all this way to talk about our differences. C'mon over here." He motioned for her to sit on his lap.

Allen fell to sleep quickly that night while Shirley wanted to savor every moment of that particular day. She was looking out over the lake when she felt a familiar pain in her fallopian tube – like the one she felt when they conceived Susan. "No way, Lord." She laughed to herself. "Is this for real? Is this David?" She laughed again. "How long will I have to keep this secret?" she asked the Lord.

Ten days after they returned there was a phone call from the doctor's office where Allen had his vasectomy done. "The results of the one-year testing are complete. You may come in and pick up the report," said the receptionist. Dr. Richards was diligent in keeping records of his patients. He did a one-year sperm count to ensure that there was minimum active sperm.

"Okay, Lord. It is time for the test. If I'm pregnant, I want proof before I get those records."

Shirley made a doctor's appointment for the next morning. The doctor returned to the room. "Yes, you are pregnant. I thought Allen had a vasectomy," he said.

"Dr. Richards is not right one hundred percent of the time. And this is one of those times," she said, feeling great vindication.

"You will have to wean yourself off the lithium immediately and I can't overemphasize the need for regular, hard exercise – enough to get your heart rate really going. Hook up with a friend you can talk to and call her if you even think you are going manic. I will see you at your regular pregnancy appointments. Good luck!"

Between the office and the car, she did a little jig. *"Yes, Lord. Thank You, Jesus. This must be David! What a wonderful God you are! Thank You! Thank You! Thank You!"*

Shirley got in the car and started driving towards Dr. Richard's office when the panic hit her. *"What if the results from Dr. Richard's test do not match the result of the pregnancy test I had? Allen will think I had a relationship outside the marriage. O God, I can't think like that. Give me the grace to get to the office with peace in my heart."* She began to take deep breaths and keep her thoughts on the goodness of God.

"Hi, I'm Mrs. Peterson," Shirley said to the receptionist. "I'm here for the results of my husband, Allen."

The nurse behind her reached for his file and started walking toward Shirley. She was reading it as she approached and then suddenly closed the file. "Dr. Richards will have to call you as soon as he comes in."

"He doesn't have to. I already know. I'm pregnant," she told the two ladies.

"I am so sorry, Mrs. Peterson," the nurse said.

"Don't be. I am absolutely delighted." And she left the office relieved that the results concurred with the findings of the pregnancy test.

*"Lord, surely Allen will see that this is your will for us. God, I can hardly contain my excitement. This is like a story right out of the Bible. Will he see it that way?"*

After the kids were in bed that night she approached him with the news. "I picked up the results of your sperm count today."

"Oh yeah. Was it next to nothing?" he asked.

"Actually the count was extremely high," she told him.

"Well, you can't keep a good guy down," he laughed. "Does that mean I have to have it done again?"

"No, it means one of your sperm met with one of my eggs and we are pregnant."

"No way!" he shouted angrily. He stood up, his face went red and his eyes looked from side to side. He leaned in at her and said sternly, "You better be getting an abortion and fast! I am not going through this again!" He stomped out the front door. She heard his truck tires peel rubber as he went down the street.

*"Lord, does this road ever get smoother?"* she asked.

*"Little One, you and Allen are like pieces of wood and sandpaper,"* He said to her. *"What happens when they are rubbed together?"* He asked.

*"Two smooth surfaces,"* she said with dawning revelation.

Allen returned about three hours later, smelling of beer. He crawled into bed and said nothing to Shirley. In fact, he didn't speak to her for a number of days. There was some functional conversation, but there was no social conversation and definitely no eye contact. When he finally spoke, he was on the opposite side of the bed with his back to Shirley. "Have you arranged for the abortion?" he asked.

"No. Would you be willing to kill Samantha or Susan? What would our lives be without either of them? Don't you think they were worth every bit of upset we went through? That's what I believe about this baby, which I believe is David, by the way. He will be worth whatever price we have to pay."

Shirley signed up for an aerobic exercise program the following Monday. They offered babysitting and held classes three times a week. In one set of exercises they clenched their fists and swung their right arm from the right to the left and then left to right. Shirley's instructor came up to her at one point and said privately in her ear. "I wouldn't want to be the person receiving the blow at the end of your arm." This was one of the few moments Shirley caught a glimpse of the depth of her anger. She knew Allen was an angry person, but she did not see that in herself. She thought about the revelation briefly, but discarded it as unimaginable. She still was a long way off from either acknowledging her anger or assessing the damage it was doing to herself and her family.

# 6

## *A New Direction*

In November 1983 Shirley had a dream in which she was full term. Paul, Susan, Samantha, and she were walking amongst the rocks by a fast moving stream. The Lord Jesus was holding Shirley's arm to help her balance. At one point she realized Allen wasn't with them. She looked to Jesus for an answer and although she didn't hear Him speak any words, she knew he was telling her Allen wouldn't be with them for some time. They continued their journey over the rocks by the stream. The dream was comforting because Jesus was with them, but the idea of being alone with all the children made her feel uncomfortable. She believed God was giving her direction for the way ahead and she kept the dream to herself.

With less than three weeks to delivery, Shirley was a very excited, expectant mom. She had remained in good health with no episodes of manic depression during this pregnancy. Allen and Shirley had remodeled their carport to give their growing family more room. Allen had accepted the coming baby and the kids were delighted as they all had a part in preparing the new baby's room in the upper part of the house.

One afternoon around 4:00 o'clock, Shirley was sitting with her next door neighbor having tea when Jane's 12-year old son Andrew came running into the kitchen, "Shirley, come quickly. Allen is beating up Paul again," he said breathlessly. She moved as fast as she could to get to the house and find Paul. In the new family room Allen was ranting about Paul ruining the new carpet. Paul was lying in a ball lifelessly on the floor. Shirley lowered her very pregnant body over Paul's and began to cry as she stroked his head. He moved underneath her to let her know he was okay. Later, Andrew told her Paul had spilled Allen's drink. Allen then flew into a rage and hit him, knocked him down, and kicked him in the back.

From within she cried out to the Lord, *"Enough. Enough, Lord. I have had enough! I don't know what we have to do, but this has got to stop! Please show me how to move away from this. Show me how to protect Paul."*

The next day Allen left for mining camp. Shirley called her pastor and told him what had happened. That afternoon he came to her house and brought three of the elders from the church. They discussed the logistics of a plan of protection for her and the three kids. They left with the promise that they would put something in place within twenty-four hours. Allen would not be home for two more days.

A family from their church took the four of them in and gave them the love and support they needed at that time. Not many days later Shirley went into labor. Fortunately, her neighbor Jane was able to be with her. She contacted Allen to let him know their son David was born. He came to visit very quickly, but he was so angry he didn't speak to Shirley. On the second visit he started talking and holding the baby. By the third visit he was talking about them all going home. She was afraid to talk to him about leaving the hospital. She had already had some time to think about what it would be like on her own with four children, one of them an infant. "What if she got sick again?" she asked herself. She was not confident that she could manage four children by herself. But the alternative held such little hope that she didn't want to think about it. So when Allen brought up the subject, she refused to talk about it. She would make that decision when she had to. Not then.

After five days in the hospital, the five of them returned to the same family who had taken them in. The couple they were with helped her think things through. She didn't know how to handle her fear because it was there for either side of the argument – to stay or to leave Allen. If she stayed, she would be constantly afraid that Allen would hurt Paul. Based on her history of illness, if she left, she could be endangering all four children. If she became ill, no one was there to get help, and therefore, her four children would be unprotected. Allen visited every day, making her decision even more difficult. When all six of them were together, the situation seemed normal – the way it should be. She was very confused about what was best for her family, and she resented the fact that she had to make this decision alone.

The dream that Shirley had the previous November had faded into the recesses of her mind. It held a provision she could not get her hands on in her current dilemma. The presence of Jesus had brought a tangible peace and security. When He helped her over the rocks, she knew He would help her through the obstacles. When she realized Allen wasn't with them, the look on His face told her all was well. Yet, she could not get the truth or the peace of the dream into her reality; so in the end, she made the wrong decision. She decided to bring all the children home and go forward with Allen, but nothing had changed between them or between Allen and Paul.

After four months of worrying if the next clash was just around the corner, Shirley was swept away with postpartum depression. Crying throughout each day, she had little or no ability to care for her children. Allen and she sent the girls to her sister-in-law's in Prince George. Paul and the baby stayed with them. Allen had to go to camp for days at a time. After two weeks, they started planning a time of rest for Paul, David, and Shirley at her sister's in Alberta. But a phone call interrupted their plans.

Her sister-in-law, Sandy, in Prince George was on the line. "I'm sorry to bother you, Shirley, but I thought it was important that you know," she said.

"What, what's wrong?" She said.

"It's Samantha. She's sick and the doctor doesn't know why. She has a fever, is dehydrated, and refuses to eat. She's losing weight rapidly. She won't respond to any treatment the doctor gives," she said.

"Okay, we'll have to get her home right away. I'll get Allen to give you a call when he gets home tonight and make arrangements for her and Susan to come home. Thanks so much for your help and this phone call," she said.

Shirley sobbed. Her little Samantha was sick and Shirley was so far away from her. "God, when will the heartache over my children ever stop?" she asked the Lord.

"*Trust in Me with all your heart, and lean not on your own understanding,* in all your ways *acknowledge Me, and I will direct your paths,*" she heard Him say. (Proverbs 3:5,6)

"O, God, I wish I could see what you see. I know you are the way," she responded.

Shirley arrived at the trailer court in Abbortsford to see Susan and Samantha outside on the porch. When Susan recognized her getting out of the car, she ran towards her and took a flying leap into her arms. “Mommy, Mommy, I missed you. I missed you so much,” she said as they kissed each other and Shirley twirled her around. Shirley gave her one more kiss, lowered her to the ground and said to her, “Okay, now I need to say ‘hi’ to Samantha,” who hadn’t moved. She was the most forlorn little two-year-old girl Shirley had ever seen. Her baggy clothes matched her unkempt, curly hair, which stood out three inches from her head. Shirley moved toward Samantha and called her by name. Samantha lowered her eyes and stood firm in her place. Her bottom lip curled down and she continued to stare at her feet. Shirley took the final step towards her and placed her hands on her arms.

“Samantha, I’m so sorry you couldn’t stay with me. Aunt Sandy called me to say you were sick and I’ve come to take you home so you can get better. Would you like to come home with me?” she asked her. Shirley began to cry to think Samantha was so wounded. Samantha began to cry. Her body remained stiff in Shirley’s arms. Although Samantha did eventually learn to trust her mom again, Shirley seldom was able to fill Samantha’s need to be affirmed and encouraged her frequently throughout her childhood years.

All six of them were together again with the normal tensions of a home with four young children with the added ever present tension between Paul and Allen. Allen and Shirley had only been married six years, but this issue between Paul and Allen had been spiraling downward from the very beginning. Every time she heard Allen raise his voice, she automatically tensed up, fearing Paul was under attack. As they neared the end of summer Shirley began to scheme for a safe place for Paul. She called her first husband Pete. He was remarried and his wife had a child Paul’s age. He was reluctant, but in the end agreed to take Paul.

"I don't want to go, Mom. I want to stay with you," Paul said.

"Honey, I can't protect you here. I could go for the groceries and come home to find you beaten up again. Paul, I can't live like this anymore," she said.

"Please don't make me go," he cried.

"I know you don't understand now, but maybe you will later on," she said.

He put his arms around her waist and continued to cry. Tears rolled down Shirley's cheeks. When Paul's sobbing and her tears subsided, she told him she would go to Vancouver with him and he would be flying on one of those big planes and live near Kanata where there was lots of snow in the winter.

Paul became extremely quiet and withdrawn in the few days before flying east. Paul would have no part of the plan. He was determined to get back with his mom. With Pete and his new family, Paul acted out in every way he knew possible. He lied; he stole and disrupted his class, and after only four weeks Pete put him on a plane and sent him back to Allen and Shirley.

Only two months went by before they were in crisis again. Allen and Paul were outside stacking wood when Allen decided Paul wasn't doing it the way he wanted. It started with yelling and cursing, but soon turned physical. Shirley grabbed the truck keys, her purse and started running down the back stairs to where they were. "STOP! STOP! ENOUGH!" she screamed. She charged past Allen and picked Paul off the ground. "C'mon, Paul. It's over. Get in the truck. I will find a safe place for you," she said with tears rolling down her face.

"Are you sending me away again?" Paul asked once the truck was moving.

"Paul, you've got to know that there is more to life than a father who belittles you and physically assaults you. I've tried to give you a life where you knew you were loved no matter what you did. I have obviously made some wrong choices and failed you," she pleaded. "I want to protect you from any more harm," she explained.

"Why do I have to go when Daddy is the bad guy?" he asked.

Shirley started to cry again. "Because I'm not strong enough to raise four kids on my own. I am so sorry I wish I could. I don't want to send you away. It's the only thing I can think to do to protect you from the abuse. I promise I'll come and see you every month once Social Services finds a family for you." Shirley had tried to set something up with a family member, but it did not work out. She felt trapped between the fear of Allen's anger and Paul's needs and by her own inability to change the situation. Her only option left to protect Paul was through Social Services.

"Paul, please forgive me. I love you so much. I am sure it doesn't feel like that right now, but I do. I love you so much," she told him.

After the paperwork at Social Services, they hugged each other and a social worker took Paul away. Shirley took the truck and drove to the hospital. She sat in the emergency ward waiting for her turn. She began to cry. She cried uncontrollably. They took her to the psych ward where she continued to sob and was unable to speak for days. She was somewhere down in a black chasm, crying out to Jesus to help her bear the pain of losing her son. There was a beam of light that reached down to her and she knew that it meant there was hope of redemption ahead. As she looked up, she saw this faint ray of light and prayed to be rescued from the chains of guilt.

When Shirley left the hospital the next week, she didn't know how Allen had coped with the children in her absence and she didn't care. She was very aware of the upward climb of forgiveness she had with Allen and herself. Her fear of him had turned to anger and her anger had the potential to be as destructive as his. Every day she had to choose to forgive. She memorized scriptures about forgiveness and said them to herself over and over again, but she easily let go of them when Allen's anger surfaced again. He didn't view his anger as inappropriate or destructive in relationships. In his mind, there was no issue. As for Shirley, she had no hope of being heard and less hope of being understood, so she kept her thoughts to herself.

Paul was placed on one of the islands in the Georgia Strait, a two ferry journey of one hour and fifteen minutes away and Shirley saw him as often as she could, no less than once a month. Sometimes she went alone and other times she took the kids. He lived with a young Christian couple who had a huge property, chickens, two golden retrievers and a lake nearby. It was an ideal set-up for the circumstance, but each visit awakened the sadness for both Paul and Shirley. She worked hard at being positive for Paul's sake, but many times missed the mark.

At the end of a fun day at the lake with the foster parents, Paul and Shirley walked ahead and Paul threw out a question Shirley did not want to hear. "When can I come home, Mom?" he asked. She hesitated and then replied, "I don't know, Paul. I don't have control over that decision anymore. I made a huge mistake and I can't fix it at this point." Tears rolled down her face. "I am sorry I have hurt you, Paul. My intent was to protect you from the abuse." Shirley grasped to find hopeful words. "You have been given a wonderful home here with Dan and Sue and a great place to live. We both have to make the most of a situation that is not our first choice. I love you and look forward to the day we can be with each other as often as we choose," she finished with a few more tears rolling down her cheeks.

Allen saw Paul as the bad kid that had to be sent away and denied responsibility for his part. In the beginning, Shirley avoided talking about Paul and any reference that he was the badly-behaved one angered her, but she kept silent. She knew she couldn't change Allen's mind about Paul, so she concentrated on the fact that she missed Paul and looked forward to the time when she would see him again. The kids helped by talking about all the details that had happened in their visits with Paul.

Shirley faithfully visited Paul once a month for the five years that Paul lived on the island except when she was in the hospital. She avoided addressing his crushed spirit and when he needed to express his pain, she diverted the conversation because she couldn't give him the outcome he so desperately wanted to hear. To cope with her own grief, she sought out quiet places and sobbed her heart out as often as the pain rose up. She read the story of Joseph from the book of Genesis over and over again and took strength from the redemptive plan of healing and forgiveness that God had for a family that went awry.

Three years after Paul left, Allen and Shirley and the three little ones moved further north up the island which was closer to where Allen worked and closer to where Paul lived. Their brand new home was on a ¾ acre lot that backed onto a forest – a paradise for the children. Shirley was thirty-seven years old and it had been a year and a half since her last episode.

Shortly after they arrived the children had a day off for teachers' professional development. It happened to fall on David's fourth birthday. Shirley went to the specialty store to get something for David and instead bought many, many items for Valentine's Day. She spent over $60 in candy and a package of cigarettes (she didn't smoke) and then announced to the children that they were going to Disneyland that very day. There was no obvious trigger for her sudden manic behavior.

"But, Mommy, we can't go today, we have to go to school tomorrow," said Samantha.

"Don't worry, Honey, I can teach you anything you miss," she replied. "Besides, how many times do you get a chance to go to Disneyland?" she asked.

Shirley and the children pulled out their summer clothing and quickly packed their bags with squeals of delight. They set off down the highway towards Victoria with the chocolate she had bought and all the pop she could find in the house. They sang and played games in the car and by the time they got to the Malahat Pass outside of Victoria, Samantha and David were asleep in the back seat.

"Hey, Susan, do you want to learn to drive the car once we get into Victoria?" she asked.

"Mom, I'm only eight years old," she responded.

"It is okay, Honey, if you grew up on a farm, you would be driving a vehicle by now," she told her.

Shirley drove to a residential area and Susan and she switched places. She propped Susan up with a cushion and pushed the seat as far forward as possible. The flat of Susan's feet were unable to reach the pedals. She steered forward for half a block, but when she turned the corner, her little arms were not strong enough and she crashed the car squarely between a tree and a fence. As soon as Shirley assessed there were no injuries, she walked all three children to a main road and flagged a taxi to take them to the ferry terminal at Swartz Bay.

He drove them to the passenger entrance and said, "That will be $36.50."

"Oh my goodness, I am so sorry. I don't have any money," she said to him. She pulled off her wedding ring and put it on the dashboard. "If you can't pawn it for $36.50, melt it down. I know there is some gold in it." She proceeded to get the children out of the taxi and move them toward the ferry entrance.

"Lady, you can't do this. You just stiffed me for $40. I should have known you were a wacko," he yelled.

"Tough luck, Mister!" Shirley yelled back and continued along the passenger entrance with the three children.

Shirley begged a man for the money to get them on the ferry. She told him she had lost her purse and she had to get to a sick aunt in Vancouver. Once on the ferry, she told her eight, six and four year olds, "Run around and have fun. I'll be sitting in this seat." They took off with great abandon. Susan came back in ten minutes and was shocked to see a cigarette in her mom's hand. "Mom, why are you smoking? You don't smoke," she asked, perplexed.

"Well, I just need it to calm my nerves," she replied.

"You said your nerves were bothering you before, but you never smoked," Susan challenged her.

"Oh, don't bother your sweet little head about it. Go find Samantha and David and bring them here," she told her. The kids played near her and then wandered off again throughout their ferry trip to Vancouver.

Shirley had no memory of how they arrived at a large department store in Burnaby from the ferry in Tsawwassen. When they walked in, she pulled out a buggy and said to the children, "Buy anything you want and put it in the shopping cart. I will pay for everything with my credit card when I get back. I'm going upstairs to get my hair done," Shirley instructed them.

Fifty minutes later she went looking for her children. A security man approached her and asked, "Do you have two girls and a boy who were shopping by themselves?" he asked.

"Yes," she said. "Where are my children?" she demanded.

"Come this way, Ma'am," he said. He took her by the arm and started leading her to the security office.

Shirley shook herself free. "Don't touch me," she said with disgust.

Once in the security office, she realized her children weren't there. She started screaming and cursing at the guards. She jumped on the console in an attempt to get past the guards and find her children. Only two men were attached to her when she reached the door. But her victory was short lived as she now faced four city policemen, two of them holding handcuffs.

"My children, they have taken my children," she pleaded. "Please help me, officer!" Shirley begged.

"Cuff her, Joe," the policeman in charge said.

Joe moved towards her. She resisted. "What kind of cop are you?" she challenged him. "Three kids are missing and all you can think about is handcuffing their mother?"

Joe handcuffed her. She was mortified that she was being treated like a criminal. Joe began pushing her towards the street door of the store. Shirley couldn't see the children, but she heard the tear filled voice of Susan. "Mommy, don't leave us," she cried.

Once out the door, Joe continued to push her towards the cruiser. He opened the back door, pushing her head down as she got into the back seat. She sat, her hands hurting with the handcuffs, facing the grill that separated the front seat from the back. Joe and his partner took Shirley to the station where she remained in a cell for many hours. Eventually, she was taken to the psychiatric ward.

This ward was different than any other Shirley had been in. She wasn't sedated when she arrived. She could hear the nurses talking to patients with compassion and understanding. She had the freedom to explore her surroundings without fear of breaking the rules. In spite of her history of long recoveries, she was ready to leave in ten days.

When they had all returned home, the stories began to trickle out. Susan, Samantha and David had gone into foster care. They were put in a home with no children. The husband watched pornographic films on a regular basis. They were put in a room with little furniture where they spent the majority of their time. They were not allowed outside. There were times when they were hungry and had no food and tired with no place to sleep except the floor. They didn't know when they would see either their mommy or daddy again. The last time they saw their mommy, she was being pushed towards the police car. Their daddy, full of his own pain and tired of picking up the broken pieces, came five days later to take them home.

Shirley was devastated that these horrible things had happened to her children, the load of guilt unbearable. If she hadn't succumbed to her madness, her children would not have suffered these indignities and ordeals, which could have long lasting effects. Deep within, she believed there had to be a way to change her life because she knew that Jesus was the truth, the light, and the way. But she had no idea where to start.

Allen and Shirley ignored the obvious need to change and they focused again on the children. When summer came they watched the schedules for the cruise ships. At night they would walk five minutes to the beach and view the lit cruise ships coming up the Georgia Strait. Allen would take one of the children fishing off the end of the nearby island in the early evening. Often as not, they would return with a salmon of five to ten pounds. Allen threw it on the grass and removed the scales with the power of the water-hose. Cooked in minutes with garlic butter, those who enjoyed salmon had a feast. The back of their property was far from their house or any neighbor. They had a fire pit at the end of it and took any occasion to have wiener and marshmallow roasts.

After Christmas 1990, Shirley invited Allen's mom to come to Campton Crossing to have a break from her usual routine. She jumped at the chance and they made plans to shop at all the second hand stores. The two took every opportunity to talk about Jesus. One morning, after Penny said goodbye to her grandkids on their way to school, she and Shirley planned to meet at a certain bus stop downtown. After her appointment, Shirley went to the designated bus stop. A bus arrived, but there was no Mom. Fifteen minutes later, another bus arrived, but no Mom.

"That doesn't make sense," Shirley said to the Lord. She walked towards her car and she said, "Lord, where is Mom?"

The Holy Spirit responded, "Penny is home."

"What is she doing there? She told me to meet her up here." Shirley replied.

Shirley got in her car and drove home; Penny wasn't there. "I feel like you are trying to tell me something, but I'm not getting it," she said to the Lord. The telephone rang. It was Allen's dad from Mayford Creek. His voice was shaken. "Shirley, your mom was stepping up onto the bus when she had a massive heart attack and collapsed. They tried to save her on the way to the hospital, but she passed away in the ambulance. She's gone!" and he began to cry.

"I can go to the hospital right now!" she replied.

"Shirley, you aren't hearing what I'm saying," he pleaded.

In silence, she tried to take in everything he had said.

"Shirley, are you there?" he asked.

"Yeah, I'm here," she replied.

"Mom has gone. I've left a message for Allen at work. I'll be calling the rest of the kids shortly," he said.

"Okay. Bye, Dad," she said.

Shirley sat on the couch, stunned. "You said she was home. I had no idea you meant Your home. Give me the grace to go through this time of mourning – the grace to tell the children. Thank you for your peace," she said to the Lord.

The children came home about an hour later. When she told them, the girls cried and snuggled into her chest. David sat across from them and curled his lip downward. After many minutes, nine year-old Samantha pulled back and said, "Grandma won't be here for the Gulf War now," and she began to cry all the more. The news of the coming Gulf War had bombarded their living room and taken over their discussion at the supper table every night. Samantha was heartbroken that she would miss sharing something so important with her Grandma.

Shirley spoke at Penny's funeral and she told the people gathered of the woman she had come to know. Penny found change difficult and she had a heart of gold. She loved her grandchildren and was always ready to help. But her real love of life came from her personal relationship to Jesus. She knew she was going to heaven for eternity, not because of what she had done, but because of what Jesus had done for her. He paid the price for her to be with Him. When Shirley and Penny were together, they had talked of the deep things of their hearts. Penny was her mother-in-law. She was her friend. She was a significant part of their family life and would be missed dearly. After Penny's death, something changed between Allen and Shirley. In some way they were further apart than before.

Campton Crossing was given to black ice conditions throughout the winter. One afternoon Susan and Shirley were returning home from shopping in their standard Ford Ranger pick-up. They came to a stop sign at the top of a very steep hill bordered by evergreen trees to the right and to the left.

Shirley put the truck in first gear and proceeded slowly forward. The road looked fine, but after five yards the truck began to slide out of control. Three sixty after three sixty they fell down the long steep hill. Susan and Shirley screamed, "JESUS! JESUS!" Then there was a thud. They were stopped. They laughed and cried at the same time. "Thank You, Jesus, for protecting us!" Their truck had spun in circles all the way down the hill and then backed into a clearing in the woods that they could not see from the top of the hill. The slowed vehicle then backed into a fallen tree to bring it to a stop. Susan and Shirley had no injuries and the truck sustained a minor dent on the back bumper. Their God was their protector even before they knew there was danger.

One time when Allen came home from camp he was extremely tired and emotionally spent. He approached the front door laden with his gear. It was locked. He kicked the front door, hoping to get Shirley's attention. She didn't hear him. The second time he kicked the door so hard, he cracked it. She heard that. He came through the door spewing profanities, boots flying, duffle bag and remaining gear rolling across the entrance way. Once he unloaded, he went straight to bed and Shirley didn't see him for the next four hours. When she was assured he wasn't coming out of the bedroom anytime soon, she began to pick up the mess. She heard the Holy Spirit ask her, "What are you doing?"

"I'm picking up the mess," she said.

"Did you make it?" He asked.

"No," she responded.

"Put it back and let Allen take care of it when he wakes up," he instructed.

To her amazement, Allen cleaned up all the mess when he woke up.

Shirley had noticed that Allen was increasingly angry towards her after his mom's death. As with Paul, the smallest incidents had the potential to incur his wrath. "Where is that insurance paper?" he barked at her one night.

"It should be in the file folder," she replied.

"Well, could you get it?" he said angrily.

Shirley looked and looked and double-checked, but could not find it. She felt the fear rising up in her. "I can't find it. I don't know why it isn't in there," she said with trepidation.

"That's it! Divorce! You are useless! You told me that you would take care of the paperwork and now you can't even do that. We are this close to a divorce," he said measuring the short distance to a split between his thumb and pointer finger. He went out the back door and slammed it as he left.

Shirley sat down on the couch, her head in her hands. *"Jesus, my Jesus. How did he get from a missing piece of paper to divorce? My God, at times like this I really hate him! I'm not saying hating him is right; I'm just telling you how I feel. Mercy, mercy, where do I go from here?" she* asked the Lord.

In the stillness, she heard Him say, *"Trust in Me with all your heart, and lean not on your own understanding; In all your ways acknowledge Me and I shall direct your paths."* (Proverbs 3:5,6)

"What does that mean, Lord, 'trust you with all my heart'? If it wasn't for trusting You, I could never have started this relationship with him or remained in it. I don't know what to do with all this anger I have towards him. He's an absolute jerk! And now he throws out the 'divorce' word! He chops at my heart like he chops at the wood for the fireplace. With precision! If it were only his and my relationship without children and without you, I would let it go in a second. I hate the way he treats me and I seem to have failed in learning to draw from you and love him. I know the path is to forgive him, but my willingness is currently at minus twenty. Lord, please take me from this hard heartedness to a place of forgiveness. I don't know the way. Please change my heart," she cried.

Allen's aggressiveness continued to grow. One day when he was angry with Shirley over something she hadn't done, he walked toward her and pinned her against the wall. "You stupid excuse for a woman. You are totally useless. I don't know what I saw in you in the first place," he yelled. Her girlfriend was shocked as she witnessed this enraged, demeaning outburst. She confirmed that Shirley's recollection of their history of events was not exaggerated.

And then came the night that altered all their lives. By nine o'clock in the evening, Shirley had tucked all three children in for the night. She read each of them a story or rubbed their backs and talked briefly with the girls. Allen sometimes participated in their nightly routines, but tonight he had started drinking early. She was exhausted, so she was in bed by 10 o'clock. She left Allen in the living room watching television and drinking beer.

At about one a.m., Shirley was awakened by laughter. She knew by the sounds that Allen had allowed Susan to get up and be with him. Furious, she charged out to the living room and pointed at Susan. "You get in your bed right now, young lady!" she yelled at her. Shirley's eyes followed her until she was in her bedroom with the door closed. Then she turned to Allen and started in on him.

"Don't you get it that you undermine my authority when you break the rules? It's one o'clock in the morning and she needs to be in school tomorrow. She needs a father, not a pal! What are you thinking?" she asked. She turned and got back into their bed.

Her heart was still pounding with anger when Allen busted through the bedroom door. He grabbed her by the throat and lifted her off the bed, her feet off the ground. She was aware that in this moment, she could die. In the silence of her heart, she cried out to Jesus and said his name over and over again to herself. Allen flung her on the bed and continued with his barrage of obscenities. He turned away from her, putting his fist straight through the wall and then through the door. In a rage he left the house, got into his truck and went speeding down the road.

Shirley lay on the bed, unsure of what had taken place. "My God, my God, help me understand what has happened," she asked.

*"If anyone fiercely assails you it will not be from Me,"* he replied. (Isaiah 54:15) NASB

"Okay, Lord, I won't put myself in that position again," she responded.

And further she heard, *"Behold, I have created the blacksmith who blows the coals in the fire, who brings forth an instrument for his work."* Isaiah 54:16.

"Lord, are You saying that there was a purpose for what just happened?" she asked.

When Allen came the next morning, she told him, "You're going to have to find a place to live. You almost killed me last night and the evidence of your rage is in the wall and the door. I'll set this next year aside for you to get help and then if nothing has changed I'll take the children and move away from the Island. It's up to you if you want your family," she said. They made some financial and visiting arrangements and he left.

In the same year that they had moved up island, Shirley had written a letter to the local newspaper of the small Newfoundland fishing village in which Paul had been born. She gave them all the details she had of Paul's birth. Paul was 13 now and had been begging her to write it. As she mailed the letter, she said to the Lord, "Jesus, I know You can find the needle in the haystack. I put this in your hands."

There was no response in the first few years. Paul's birth mother had been told that she had a girl, and it wasn't until 1991 after much searching she discovered the province had no record of her ever giving birth to a girl. One of her sisters who had read the original letter to the editor in 1988 reminded Sara of it and its similarities to Sara's baby except that it was a boy. Sara contacted the editor, received Shirley's details and phoned Shirley in January 1992. Sara and Shirley talked a number of times in the ensuing months and Paul and Shirley made plans to go to Newfoundland in mid-May.

Sara and her husband picked Paul and Shirley up at the airport May 12, 1992, days after Allen and she had separated. Sara had no doubt which passenger was her son as he was the spitting image of his biological father. The first few days they visited in a little fishing village with Sara, her husband and their son. On the fourth day, Sara, Paul, and Shirley drove to the village where Paul was born and where all of Sara's nieces, nephews, sisters, and mother lived. Paul appreciated the experience of being surrounded by people who looked like him. Shirley talked with her sisters and mother while Paul was off with his cousins. She dodged some of their questions as she wasn't ready to divulge much information. She was still processing some of the events herself. Paul felt divided in his loyalties between a family he knew and a family he was attached to by blood. He did not keep up contact when they returned to B.C., but his little brother would one day search him out and the two would become good friends.

As the months rolled on, Shirley saw no hope that Allen and she could live together safely. The consequences of their separation began to tell in other ways. David was much bigger than children his age and he used his size to bully them. His aggressive behavior had started from the time he entered school. He had been expelled from a Christian school the year before and during their separation, he revved up his belligerent behavior and was suspended several times from a public school. He had been at a boy's camp on Kelly Island when Shirley received an angry call. "Mrs. Peterson, David's behavior has been absolutely unacceptable. I will put him on the 7:05 p.m. ferry. You need to have someone there to meet him," she said.

As Shirley stood looking at Kelly Island waiting for his ferry to arrive, she began talking to the Lord, *"Okay, so this hasn't worked out. David needs a time to heal. This situation is too volatile for him. Where do we go?"* Allen and she had exhausted their resources trying to fix the marriage. The toll was visible on all of them. She knew that they couldn't do life this way anymore. She could no longer ignore the winds of change that had been blowing for some time. Edmonton came on the radar. The tears rolled down her face.

*Your word says,* 'For your Maker is your husband!' (Isaiah 54:5) *I can't do this unless You are my husband. I mean for real. I will have to make a lot of decisions and I don't want to be making them by myself. I don't want to be alone. Your word also says,* 'All your children shall be taught by the Lord, And great shall be the peace of your children.' (Isaiah 54:13) *These can't be just words. I need them to be more than true. I need You to care for my children beyond anything I could do. Will you be my husband and take care of the details of my life?"*

David came walking up from the ferry. He was never much for hugs. "I love you, David," she said and pointed towards the car. As they drove home that night she had all the evidence sitting beside her that it was time for a new direction. David was on a path of destruction at the age of eight and she did not want to see her second son's life crushed by her passivity.

# 7

## *Jesus as Her Husband*

Shirley met with Allen the next day. "Allen, this isn't working. David's behavior is getting worse. You give your children whatever they want and there is no discipline. You seem quite happy with the situation the way it is and I see no desire in you to change," Shirley said.

"Shirley, I can't live with your mental illness. When I come home from work, I don't know if you will be there or where you and the children will be. I don't know if I am going to lose my job because I have to make arrangements for the children. I never know what is going on when you have these fits," he replied.

"And if I had cancer would you feel the same?" she asked.

"Cancer isn't anything like bi-polar disorder. If you had cancer at least I would know where you are. We would be making decisions about the children together. It's the not knowing that I can't handle," he said.

They sat in silence for several minutes. "I think the children and I should leave as soon as possible," she started.

"I sure don't like losing the children, but I can't see any other way out of this," he said as his eyes watered. "We can put the house up for sale and split any profit fifty-fifty after all the bills are paid. I will support the children monthly until they are eighteen."

He made it sound like the separation was for good. Shirley couldn't deal with that emotionally at the time. She put it on the shelf; she would face it later.

They had an offer on their house almost immediately, but it was conditional upon the sale of the purchaser's home. Shirley began to prepare mentally for the move to Edmonton. She wanted to line up housing, schooling and everything else she could nail down before taking the whole family there. As she was sharing her ideas with her friends Gwen and Thomas, Gwen reached across the table and took her hand. "We can help you financially with that. Right, Thomas?" she asked her husband. "Sure, Honey," he replied.

Shirley made plane reservations for David and herself to visit Edmonton. As she had burnt some bridges earlier, she had no offers of accommodation from her sister or her friend who lived in Edmonton. With less than twenty-four hours before departure, they had no place to stay and she had booked the trip for a week. "Lord, we need a place to stay. I can't do this alone. Please, show yourself as my husband," she prayed. Shirley was going into the bank to get some cash for their trip when she literally bumped into her friend Mary from church.

"When are you going to Edmonton?" she asked.

"We're leaving tomorrow, but we don't have a place to stay yet."

"And you are leaving tomorrow?" she asked.

"Yes," she replied.

"I have a cousin who lives in the west end. Let me call her tonight when I get home from work. Maybe she is able to help or maybe someone she knows could help. I'll call you as soon as I have talked with her," she said.

That night her friend Mary called at 9:30 p.m. "My cousin Bonnie and her family would love to have you and David and are quite willing to help you with the details. Do you have a ride from the airport?" she asked.

"Yes, I'm renting a car. I've been to Edmonton a few times. I'm sure with instructions, I'll be able to find Bonnie's place. Edmonton is laid out on a grid, isn't it?" she asked.

It was a smooth, short flight and David was engrossed in his comic book. Their luggage came out quickly and they were on their way to pick up their rental car. It was a Toyota Tercel. Nothing fancy, but very functional – just as Shirley had requested. It was time to begin their new adventure.

"Okay, Father God, this is it. Lead us and guide us. Reveal all the details to us. Give me a clear path to Bonnie's house," she prayed.

"Who are you talking to?" asked David.

"Jesus," she replied.

"Do you really believe in him?" David asked her.

"Yes, David. I really believe in Jesus and his desire to help us. One day you will know how much He loves you and wants to be your closest friend," she told him.

"Doubt it," he replied.

Shirley followed the signs to the West Edmonton Mall and she knew she was only a few minutes away. Soon they were in front of the house. She rang the doorbell and waited nervously. "Bonnie?" she asked. The woman nodded. "I am Shirley Peterson and this is my son, David," Shirley said, extending her hand. "Thank you so much for helping us out," she said awkwardly.

Within two days Shirley had secured a place for her family to live. On the third day she spoke with the principal of a nearby Christian school and told him of their circumstances. He welcomed her and Shirley enrolled the children. The school was a 25-minute walk from their house. The next day Shirley and David registered at a doctor's office and learned the procedures for health care in a new province. They went to the West Edmonton Mall to look around and hopefully have some fun. David had only been four the last time he had been there. As an eight- year old he wanted to go on the rides, but rides made his mom sick and Shirley had no intentions of going on them.

"So you have finally found a purpose for your sisters," she said.

"What do you mean?" he asked.

"Well, you will need them to get on these rides. I'm sure they will comply," she said. "When we come back as a family, you'll have lots of opportunities to go on the rides and maybe all of us can go to the water park. There must be some little slides for me," she laughed.

Shirley and David returned home. He told the girls some of the things he had seen at the West Edmonton Mall and they schemed together what they might do when they arrived. Samantha experienced some sadness about leaving, but was very excited about the changes ahead. David had no close friends and once he had seen Edmonton, he was ready to go. Susan was twelve and her life was her friends. She had always had a special bond with her dad. This move would be difficult for her. Paul decided he would stay on Vancouver Island for a little longer, saying he might move to Edmonton later. He wasn't ready to go when they were.

The house sold only because Allen sacrificed his gain from their house and bought the buyer's old house. This enabled them to leave sooner rather than later. Shirley didn't know if he wanted them gone or he thought it was the best decision for his family.

Finally, they arrived in Edmonton. They had another twenty-four hours before their friends would arrive with their 5-ton truck loaded with their furniture. The kids unpacked their suitcases and laid out their sleeping bags on the living room floor. They walked over to the Westmount Plaza to pick up some food and then Shirley hit a wall of exhaustion. "Look kids, I've got to get some sleep. If anyone wakes me up and especially if they are fighting, you will see a very angry mother. Read your books or play the games you brought, but BE QUIET!!!!" she said emphatically. Shirley took her sleeping bag into one of the bedrooms and after a few tears she fell asleep for a number of hours.

Their friends Glen and Andrea arrived the next day. Together, they all unpacked the truck. Shirley was so comforted to see familiar faces in this land of new beginnings. When they left the next morning, she felt like they were cutting the last tie with B.C. and what was known to them. From now on it would be an adventure with God and at times with Him alone.

Shirley decided not to work in the first season. She had received enough money from the house that it was feasible to make this choice – scary, but feasible. She saw that her children had been adversely impacted by the series of events. Weighing their emotional stability against a steady income, she decided she was willing to gamble. It was one of those places she could not see around the corner, but she had learned to count on Jesus when she was blind.

It turned out to be the right decision because both David and Susan needed some extra help in adjusting. Calls from the principal's office began almost immediately. David was physical with the other children and had no regard for the rules. Being a bully was paying off for him. He liked the fact that kids his age were afraid of him. At home, he would go after Samantha when he thought Shirley wouldn't see him, but if he challenged Susan, he would get the worst of it. The principal worked painstakingly with him with Shirley's cooperation for the next year. There were many, many meetings with the principal, David, and herself. David either refused to engage, or said that he would change and then didn't. Success for Shirley was a day when she wasn't called to the principal's office.

Shirley knew that David was working out his emotions of the break-up of his family, as were the other two. Unfortunately, his search to understand himself had horrible consequences for others, including Samantha. Shirley often prayed that God would give her a determined spirit against any kind of adversity in her life. Samantha, her social butterfly, made friends quickly and was off doing some activity regularly with them. She was sad, missing her friends from back home at times, but settled into Edmonton more easily than her siblings.

Susan fell into a serious depression. Getting her out of bed became a challenge for both Susan and her mother. Susan appeared drugged. Resetting the alarm, Shirley raising her voice, threatening, coaxing and taking away privileges had minimal effect. One morning while Susan was still in bed, Shirley sat on the couch and spoke to her Faithful One. *Father, I don't know what to do for her. Please guide me.* Shirley began to think about the fact that Susan's strength had always been her athleticism. In her mind, Shirley could see her playing volleyball and basketball. She left Susan in bed and made her way to the principal's office. He advised her to see the coach of the volleyball team as that was the season's sport.

"Hi, my name is Shirley Peterson and I have recently brought my family here from British Columbia. I have one daughter who is finding the transition especially difficult. She has always excelled in sports and I was wondering if there was a place for her on your volleyball team?" she asked.

"I'm sorry, I picked the team last week," he replied.

"Could you please make an exception? This is really important to her health and her family's welfare," Shirley begged.

"I wish I could help, but I can't see a way," he replied.

"Could you just put her on the bench and tell her she might not get a chance to play. At least she could practice and get to know the girls," she pleaded.

"Well, I suppose I could try that. We have a practice today at 3:30. Have her come and we'll see how it goes," he concluded.

Susan was reluctant to be with the girls. She was the outsider with little hope of fitting in. But a little spark ignited with the possibility of playing a sport. She hadn't played much volleyball, but she quickly picked up every game she tried. Volleyball was no exception. When it came to playing the games, often at least one girl was not able to play. This enabled Susan to test her skills. She was good and the team was glad to have her. She was never one of the girls socially, but when it came to the game, she was one of the team. Susan left the deep sadness and despair behind as she reached for different sports, especially softball in which she excelled. However, she would work out emotional issues she had as a teenager for many years to come.

As for Shirley, she waited until all the children were in school and had a regular time talking with her Lord. She talked about her children's needs, her need for a job when it was time, and a permanent car. She was only renting one for the first month until she had the kids settled and then she would follow up on Bonnie and Mike's lead to the car rental company. When she arrived the man said, "If there is anything broken or that needs to be attended to, the repair is included in the price," he said.

"What is the price?" She asked.

"$7,500.00. Every car is the same price. Just come out back and choose the one you want," he said as he led her to the back lot. Her eyes fell on a sea of Toyota Tercels. "I will be in my office. Let me know if there is one you are interested in," he said as he left.

*Father, Father, how do I choose?* she asked.

Shirley heard the word 'odometer'.

She was so excited with the reality that God was willing to help her with such a mundane detail. She checked the odometer of every single car and chose the car with the least mileage. It was black and had a broken window and a few spots that needed repairing. She told Joe which car she wanted and he said he would call her as soon as it was ready. She picked it up two days later all cleaned and looking like new.

During her time of not working, she frequently passed a Christian bookstore located in an otherwise residential area. Each time she passed it, she felt compelled to pray for the owner, for the business and for the construction that was underway there. One morning the Holy Spirit said, "I want you to give $5,000 to the owner of that business." She sat on the couch and thought about it.

*Lord, you know it's not about the money. I know it's not mine and that you have only entrusted it to me – just like my children. But I would feel so embarrassed to have to say to a stranger,* 'God told me to give this to you.' *The owner will think I'm nuts!* She laughed. *So I need you to do something in my heart to change this.* She thought of what the Lord was asking her to do and she was refreshed by much laughter. She remembered the scripture about the Lord loving a cheerful giver.

More than a week passed before she got up the courage to go to the Christian bookstore with check in hand. She must have said, 'Jesus, help me' at least thirty times between the car and the store. Inside, a twenty–something year old approached Shirley.

"May I help you," she asked.

"Yes, I am looking for the owner," Shirley replied.

"I am the owner. My name is Stacie. What can I do for you?"

"Could we talk in your office?" Shirley asked.

They sat down across from each other and Shirley began.

"Stacie, I have been praying for your business for some time now and I believe the Lord instructed me to give this to you," she said as she handed her the check.

Stacie looked at it and then looked even closer. Tears started to fall down her face and then she collapsed in weeping.

*O Lord, what do I do now? Is this a bad thing?* Shirley thought to herself.

Stacie composed herself and told her the story. "My construction manager told me if I couldn't give him $5000 by the end of this week, he would have to stop construction. I did not have it and I have been crying out to the Lord. You are a stranger and you walk in and bring the answer to my prayers!"

"I'm so relieved you actually needed it and that I had heard the Lord," Shirley confessed.

Together they laughed and shed tears of joy.

"I will pay you back as soon as possible," she promised.

"I believe you," she replied.

Four months later as Shirley was having her quiet time, she began to think again of Stacie. She prayed for her and her needs and then decided to phone her and ask her what in particular she could be praying for.

"Hi, Stacie. It's Shirley," she started.

"How have you been doing?" she asked.

"Well, when I was praying this morning, I started thinking of you. Is there something specifically I should be praying for you?" Shirley asked.

"As a matter of fact, there is. I need to hire a bookkeeper," she said.

Shirley's heart began to beat a little faster. "I'm a bookkeeper. Could I apply?" she asked.

"Of course. Bring in your resume and I'll go over it with my overseer," she said.

Shirley sat back down on the couch and tears of joy streamed down her face. *You knew it was time to go to work. You knew my need and her need and you have worked it all together. I haven't even got to the point of looking for a job. My God, my God, you are so incredible. What a father! What a husband! I feel so humbled by your love.* Shirley was able to work her choice of hours, drop off her kids at school, go to work and leave when school was finished. She was able to be present for her children's extracurricular activities.

In that first year especially, she experienced the reality of God's provision in all the details of her life - a home, car, job, and Christian fellowship. Soon after she arrived in Edmonton she sought out a Vineyard church. She had been greatly impacted by their teaching and their presentation of the scriptures in relationship to the persons of the Father, Son and Holy Spirit. It was at this church that she was introduced to the idea of small groups. Five hundred people attended each Sunday, so a small group of fifteen was ideal for forming meaningful relationships and learning how to love one another. They became a close-knit family and experienced an openness to the Holy Spirit.

Worship lasted at least an hour. For Shirley, it was like being transported to heaven. Not so for her children. While she worshipped totally enthralled, her children sat on the pew behind her, physically fighting. No stern word affected them. She was in her most vulnerable place. She would do anything to be in corporate worship. One Sunday afternoon driving home from church, she said to the kids, "You know the scriptures say that God is the father of the fatherless? Well, I have decided to entrust you into His care. None of you are allowed to come to church anymore until you have decided you want to be there. However, if I come home after church and anyone has hurt another or made a mess, then that person will come to church with me the following Sunday. Got it?" she asked.

"Got it," they chimed.

Shirley didn't recall having to haul anyone off to church that year. About six months later, Susan asked if she could join her mother at church and then in another month or so, Samantha wanted to join them. David never came back to church.

In the four years they were in Edmonton, Allen often came to visit when the kids had a tournament. Susan played softball on an 'A' team and he would drive or fly to be with her in tournaments across Alberta. David played hockey locally and Allen was there as often as he could be. Thirteen months into their time there, he said he wanted to come for a visit. His voice was much softer than usual and when he arrived his eyes told Shirley that he hadn't just come to see the children. He was flirtatious and asked her to go for a walk – something he never did back in Campton Crossing. He started talking about what it would be like to be back together. She told him it was too soon, but if he wanted to come and visit them on a regular basis that would be fine with her. For five months, he came once a month, but it was a honeymoon type relationship.

On one Easter Sunday, they were preparing to go to David's final game of a tournament. All five of them were at the table for breakfast when someone spilled milk all over Allen. He jumped up from his seat and began yelling, "What is this? I can't even sit down for a meal without one of you little suckers making a mess all over me!" he said as he picked up a tea towel and started towards the bathroom.

"Finish your breakfast and we'll get ready for the game," Shirley told the kids.

"I don't want to go," Susan said.

"Me neither," said Samantha.

"Okay," she said to the girls. "David, you finish up and I'll take you to the rink. You don't have to rush. We still have twenty minutes."

Shirley went to see what had happened to Allen. He was lying on the back bed, arms folded, face reddened, eyes closed but fluttering. "Are you going to David's game?" she asked.

There was no response. She closed the door and went back to attend to the kids.

Shirley drove David to the rink and watched him on the ice from the top of the stands, thinking about what had happened at home. It did not seem right that David did not have his dad watching the game. She ran out and jumped in the car to go get Allen. She found him in the same position. "It's obvious you aren't sleeping. David's game starts in ten minutes. C'mon let's go," she said and left the room. He didn't follow.

She returned. "Do you remember what it felt like when you were doing something important to you and you wanted your dad there to see you? The most important thing to David right now is to look in the stands in the arena and see his dad. You have come all this distance. You only have a few blocks more to go. Your son needs to see you at his game today. I will wait in the car," she said.

Five minutes later he sat down in the passenger seat, arms folded. No words were spoken on the way to the rink. He sat at the same height from the ice as Shirley did, but thirty feet to her right. After the game, they took David home. Allen spoke a few encouraging words to David for his efforts. Then Allen and Shirley set out for his friend's on the other side of Edmonton on the way to the airport.

In the car on the way over, Shirley tried to put the feelings of her heart into words he would hear and understand. "Well, Allen, the next move is up to you. From my perspective, you need to apologize to me and to your children for your behavior. If you get on that plane today with your pride intact and no restoration, the chances of this family making it together are slim to none. Cursing, yelling, and belittling are the behaviors of an undisciplined man. We need you to lead this family as a mature, loving father and husband who puts the welfare of his family first, even before his own needs or desires. The choice is yours. End of sermon," she concluded. His face reddened and his arms folded more tightly than before as he glared ahead at the roadway before them.

Shirley spoke silently to her God. *I surrender to you, Lord. I have done everything I know to do. If I have said or done anything to hinder the process of healing between us, I ask that you show me and that You would redeem it. It feels good not to be afraid of him. I don't ever want to go there again. Thank You for Your presence now.*

They arrived at Allen's friend's house fifteen minutes later. Becky greeted him with her usual pinching of the cheeks and "Petesie, Petesie, what is the matter for you, Petesie?" she asked in her thick Polish accent. She started up a conversation with Shirley about the children, but her attention was quickly drawn to her long-time friend in the far room. "Petesie, what's the matter for you? Why you pouting? You look like you have lost your good friend. Tell Auntie Becky. You can always tell Auntie Becky," she persisted. His face reddened and he said nothing.

Becky and Shirley were lost again in conversation, but her heart turned back to her friend again. She began to cook up her latest batch of perogies. Looking at Allen, she said, "Okay, Petesie. I will get some perogies going here and see if we can't cheer you up a bit. These ones have bacon too!" she said as she continued to prepare the meal. He spoke a few words to Becky as they ate and very little afterwards. As they were leaving, she put her hands on his shoulders and looked him in the eyes and said, "Whatever decision you are making, choose wisely. Don't let that anger of yours be the deciding factor." Then she hugged him and kissed him on each cheek and wished him well.

Allen and Shirley returned to the snowy streets in Edmonton on their way to the airport. Riding in silence, Shirley went through all the details in her mind hoping to think of something significant to say. There was nothing. He said nothing. They arrived at the airport. He took his luggage from the trunk of the car, turned his back to Shirley, and walked into the departure lounge. Two months later, a mutual friend contacted Shirley to let her know he was living with a woman and he was very happy.

# 8

## *Too Many Children*

*There is a fire in the living room. Get out!* Paul opened the door to the living room and it was engulfed in flames. In the middle of the night after drinking with his friends, he awoke suddenly and distinctly heard these words. He went back into his bedroom and made his way out the ground floor apartment. The next day he told Shirley, "Mom, that voice I heard was a voice of an angel. I never wake up in the middle of the night, let alone on a night when I have been drinking." And looking up to heaven he said, "Thank you, God, for saving my life, again."

Three months earlier, Paul had moved to Edmonton, found work and lived nearby his family in an apartment with his friend Jack from Campton Crossing. That night Jack and his girlfriend were smoking on the couch, not knowingly dropped an ash and left. The incident really shook Shirley, but she was so glad to have Paul close to her again.

Susan gravitated to the two least desirable girls in the Christian high school. Anna and Cissy wore black leather clothing, way too much make-up, had spiky hair and chewed gobs of gum. Everything about them reflected rebellion - rich girls who got whatever they asked for. One night Shirley followed the three of them from their home to Anna's. One of them had a bag and Shirley suspected there was beer in it. They went inside and Shirley knocked on the door. Anna's mom opened the door and said, "You must be Susan's mom."

"Yes, I am. I followed the girls here and I suspect there is beer in that bag," she said.

Anna's mom looked in the bag and pulled out a beer. "Well, would you look here? Don't tell me, you are one of those goody two shoes? The girls just want to have a little fun. Lighten up, Sister," she said.

"The girls are fifteen. It is illegal for them to be drinking. It's an offense for you to be supplying it to them," Shirley said.

"Oh, you are way too serious, Honey," she replied.

Shirley looked at Susan and headed toward the door. "Susan, come," she said sternly.

"But, Mom, I want to be with my friends," she said.

"Susan, now!" she repeated herself. Susan followed her mother reluctantly.

As they walked along the back lane to their house, Shirley broke the silence. "You are making a poor choice hanging around with those girls. You could be ruining your life with them as friends. They are on a path of destruction. You need to do what you know is right. You need to choose a different path. I can guide you, but you have to choose," she said. Susan remained silent as they entered the house and she went to her room.

A week later Shirley heard Susan on the phone for a long time, so she knew she was talking to a friend from Campton Crossing. When she finished, Susan came to talk to her on the couch, "Mom, Christine needs help. Can we help her?" she asked.

Christine's mom had a mental illness and had always relied on Christine to take care of her and Christine's younger brother. Social Services had stepped in and were looking for placements for her and her brother. Susan snuggled up to her mom. "Christine is going to be put in a foster home and she is very afraid where she will end up. She wants to know if she can come and live with us. Please, Mom, I will share my room with her. I will do whatever it takes to make it work," she pleaded.

"I would like to help Christine. You know I really like her. Let me think about it and pray about it," she answered. She left the room and returned after half an hour. "Ask Christine to get a number for the agency that finances her," she requested.

"Yeah, Mom, you're the greatest," Susan squealed in delight.

"Not so fast. We need to get a few things sorted out before there is any decision," she said.

Shirley made all the necessary calls for Christine and she was in their home within the month. She sat the girls down on the couch and explained to them, "Christine, I have allowed you to come because I love you and want to see you finish your education. It is your responsibility to be to school on time and work hard to finish high school. Susan, the same goes for you. You need to co-operate with Samantha and David and give them help when they need it," she instructed them.

"Oh, yes, I will do whatever you say," Christine said.

"Me too, Mom," Susan chimed in. And off they went to sort out Susan's room.

Unbeknownst to Shirley, Christine joined Susan's friends and the four of them formed a gang at their local public high school; verbal abuse was their weapon against a rival group of girls who had established their toughness long before Susan and her friends had arrived. One day, it went beyond words and Susan and the main girl from the other side set a time to meet in the courtyard and fight it out with fists.

The din from the crowd was deafening, but Susan and her enemy glared at each other while lining up the next punch. Both were bleeding when a teacher realized what was happening and came to break it up. The teacher took them to the principal's office, and Susan and the girl were suspended for a number of days.

"Oh my goodness, what happened to you?" Shirley asked when Susan walked through the door.

"This girl at school called me names one too many times, and I decided not to take her bad attitude any longer. I beat her up. She won't be on my back any time soon," she told her mother.

"Susan, since when did you decide it was okay to use another human being for a punching bag?" Shirley asked her.

"Since she started using me for a target with her nasty tongue," Susan responded as she moved towards her room.

*My God, my God, where is my beautiful-hearted daughter? How long will it be before she gets off this path and gets back into your arms?*

The words from Isaiah floated through Shirley's mind, "*O you afflicted one, tossed with tempest, and not comforted, behold I will lay your stones with colorful gems and lay your foundations with sapphires. I will make your pinnacles of rubies, your gates of crystal, and all your walls of precious stones. All your children shall be taught by the Lord, and great shall be the peace of your children.*" (Isaiah 54:11 -13)

"Thank you, Lord, for your word. My hope is in you," she said to her loved one.

Shirley found Paul's friend Jack living in his car in extreme cold temperatures some months later. She invited him to come stay with the family until he found a place to live. This was the mistake that would unravel Shirley's cozy little nest.

Susan, Christine, and Jack started hanging around together, and Shirley was increasingly uncomfortable with the new development. One day Shirley saw Christine put something in her back pocket.

"Christine, what did you just put in your pocket?" she asked.

"Nothing," she said.

"I just saw you put something in your pocket. Show me, please," Shirley requested.

Christine pulled it out and placed it in her hand. "It looks like a scrunched up cigarette with no filter," Shirley said.

"Yep, that's what it is," the teen replied.

"I used to roll my own cigarettes and they never looked like that. What is it, Christine?" Shirley asked again.

She lowered her eyes and quietly said, "Marijuana."

"Where did you get it?" Shirley asked.

Christine continued staring at the floor and remained silent. Shirley waited and waited.

"Was it Jack?" she asked.

Her lip quivered and finally she said, "Yes."

When Jack came in from work that night, Shirley told him she wanted to talk to him privately.

Once inside his room, she pulled out the joint and asked, "Did you give this to Christine?"

He lowered his eyes and said, "Oh no, Shirley. I would never do that."

"You are lying, Jack. You need to pack your bags and be gone in the morning," she commanded.

"You're wrong about me. Christine probably got it at school," he said in his defense.

"No more, Jack. I've had my suspicions about your behavior a number of times. I said you could stay here until you found a place, but you are too comfortable here to look. It's time for you to go," she replied.

Jack had only been with them for four months. He was a likeable young man, but his sense of right and wrong was very different than Shirley's and what she wanted to teach her children. She felt guilty that he had to leave. She hated relationship failures. But this step with Jack was only the beginning.

Even before Jack left, Christine had begun a habit of sleeping in and being late or missing school.

"Christine, this is not acceptable," Shirley said one afternoon when she came home from work. This was not what I agreed to. You need to make a change immediately," she said.

"Yeah, yeah," Christine replied as she made her way to the shower.

But it happened again, and again and again. One morning it all came to a head. Shirley was yelling and screaming at her to get to school and Christine was ignoring her. Suddenly Christine turned to face her and yelled curses, accusations and threats. Shirley was stunned. In a quiet voice she said, "Well, if you think it is okay to talk to me like that, it's time for you to leave."

Christine made arrangements to drive back to Campton Crossing with Jack. Again Shirley felt guilty that Christine was leaving. Shirley asked herself if she had done everything she could to make this relationship work. Had she been too strict? Had she been too lenient? And now Shirley had no control over Christine's choice of companion with whom she would drive to Campton Crossing. Questions plagued her mind.

Shirley decided to take a break, but instead had a breakdown. She drove to Whistler along with a few friends from church to attend a gathering of Christians focused on praying for Canada. They stayed in a rented mansion in Blueberry Hill. The only thing between them and the Conference Center was the golf course with a pathway at the end of it running parallel to the highway. They registered and went for a walk in the village and then back to enjoy their beautiful accommodation, hot tub included. The Friday night gathering was a time of glorious worship, dancing, and very little speaking. Tribes from various indigenous groups were dressed in full regalia. Shirley, knowing she was of Ojibway descent, was fascinated with their dress and had conversations with a number of them. For Shirley, it was a wonderful time of refreshing and she did not realize she was beginning to go high.

Shirley slept little and the next morning she joined with the thousands at the Conference Center for the ceremonies of the day. While the events of the day were whirling along, her mind was whirling away from reality and she became manic. She was doing everything possible to draw attention to herself: dancing, singing erratically, and making suggestive gestures to married men from other countries. Suddenly she was grabbed by four security men – one on each leg and arm and she was carried out of the building. They lowered her on the concrete, stripped her of her name-tag and the registration toggle around her neck. One man leaned over her face and in a disgusted tone said, "May you burn in hell!" They returned to the meeting.

As Shirley lay there on the ground, she spoke to Jesus: *I don't understand why that man is so angry with me. And I am not going to hell! He is wrong! What an evil man!*

Shirley sat up and assessed her situation. She had left her shoes in the Conference Center. The valley trail was made of gravel, not paved as in later days. She still had to make her way back to Blueberry

Hill – a twenty-minute walk. She started tiptoeing down the trail. Her feet hurt with every step and it was getting dark. "Jesus, could you please send someone down this path to walk with me? I can't see a thing," she said.

Thirty seconds later a man in his mid-twenties came by. "Hi there. Can you help me? I can't see in the dark and I am barefooted and my feet hurt," she made her plea.

"Sure, put your hand on my arm and I will lead you," he said.

When she was steadied she asked him, "Has anyone ever told you how much Jesus loves you?" she asked.

"No, not really," he replied.

"OUCH!" she cried as she stepped on the stones. "Did you know that God is a holy, ouch, God and that if you had one sin in your life and you tried to get near Him – poof – you would be dead? So God made a way for you, ouch, to get close to Him because He loves you and me. He sent Jesus who knew no sin. He paid the price, ouch, ouch and ouch, by suffering and dying for our sins. When God looks at us, He sees Jesus and welcomes us. Ouch, ouch, all you have to do is believe. Do you believe?" she asked.

He gave a little laugh and said, "I have never thought of it before," he responded.

"Will you think about it?" she asked.

He laughed again. "Sure," he said, "I will think about it."

"Now tell me the truth. Are you an angel in disguise?" she asked.

Again he laughed "No, I am not an angel," he said.

They came to the pavement of the road to Blueberry Hill. "I am going further, so good luck on the rest of your journey," he said."

"Think about what I said," she yelled as he went on his way.

Shirley didn't sleep much that night and the next day she wandered around the village as she was barred from the conference. "Did they throw you out of the conference too?" she heard a voice behind her. She turned to see a hippie-like character.

"Yes," she replied.

"They thought I was a warlock. I just came to protest this stupid Christian gathering. They deny freedom of speech," he said. Shirley turned and walked away from the weirdo. She wanted to be as far away from him as possible. It was a beautiful, warm, balmy day. She soaked up the rays as she walked towards the mountains.

The next day they drove back to Edmonton. Even with little sleep the night before, she was talkative as they drove through the mountains; in her mind all was well. As her friend drove towards the hospital in the west end of Edmonton, a panic enveloped Shirley. She saw her son Paul having a smoke outside the emergency doors. It was a set-up! As the vehicle slowed, she opened the door and jumped out. Yelling and screaming, she ran across the hospital grounds. No way was anyone going to get her through the doors to the psych ward. Paul was running in pursuit of her. "Mom…… stop!" he yelled at her. She turned to answer him, tripped and fell. He helped her up. "It is okay, Mom. You can get help in here," he said.

"No, Paul, you're wrong. They will drug me and put me away in a room with just a mattress on the floor. I won't be able to see out the window on the door because it will be filled with mesh wire. The outside windows will be blocked with plywood. There will be no blankets and no mirrors to look at myself. There will be nothing to do for hours and days. I am not going in there and if you try and force me, I will fight you!" she shouted.

"Okay, Mom. Sit here on the grass. Will you stay here while I go talk to the doctor?" he asked.

"Okay, Paul. But I am not going in," Shirley stated.

"Promise you will stay here?" he asked.

"Don't let anyone else come for me or I will run," she declared.

"Okay, Mom," he said and he walked towards the hospital. He spoke with Dr. Brown. "Look, my mother has had some horrible experiences with psychiatric wards. If I could bring her in and show her the bed she will be sleeping in, the kitchen area, just like you showed me earlier, I am sure she will be fine," he proposed to the doctor.

"We could try it," he responded.

"Here's the kicker," Paul said.

"What do you mean?" the doctor asked.

"Would it be possible to clear all hospital staff in this area while we do this? If she sees staff, she will think I have betrayed her and she will yell, punch, bite or whatever else she needs to do to get out of here. She doesn't need to be any more upset than she already is," Paul pleaded.

The doctor talked with the head nurse then came back to Paul. "Stay with your mom until I give the signal. Then bring her in," he instructed.

"Thanks, Doctor," he said with relief and ran across the lawn to where Shirley was sitting.

"Mom, I have talked with the doctor and he is going to let you come inside and see your bedroom, the kitchen, the living room and the entire area where you will be staying. It's not anything like that horrible hospital you were in before. Will you let me show it to you?" he asked.

"I don't know, Paul. They could trick me," she replied.

"I won't trick you, Mom. I will be right with you," he assured her.

"I am really afraid. Will you hold my hand?" she asked.

"Yes, Mom. I'll hold your hand. And I won't leave you until you are settled. C'mon, Mom, you need to get help and I can't give you the help you need," he said.

"Okay, but don't let go of my hand!" she demanded.

Paul saw the doctor signal. Shirley and Paul made their way towards the hospital. She squeezed Paul's hand so tightly it hurt. No one was in the hallway. No one was at the nurses' desk. Her mind was telling her there was a bunch of people just waiting to jump her around the other corner.

"It is okay, Mom. It's just a little bit further. You are doing great. Only one more hallway and I can show you your bedroom," Paul reassured her. "See, this will be your bedroom - almost as nice as your bedroom at home. And look, there is the kitchen and living room and everything else just like I told you," he said. "What do you think?" he asked.

"Okay, I think," her voice quivered. She could hear footsteps approaching. Her breathing rate increased.

"Mom, Dr. Brown is coming to speak to you," Paul said.

"Mrs. Peterson, I am Dr. Brown," he said as he extended his hand. "I am sorry you are not feeling well. How many days has it been since you have had a full night's rest?" he asked.

"Four or five. Maybe more," she responded.

"Mrs. Peterson, you need your sleep in order to recover. Will you allow me to give you some medication that will cause you to sleep?" he asked.

"No, no needles!" she resisted.

"MOM! Do you want to get home with the kids?" Paul asked impatiently.

"Yes," she answered.

"Then, please, TAKE THE NEEDLE!" Paul yelled.

Shirley started crying. "Okay, but don't yell at me."

"Paul is going to leave now, Mrs. Peterson. He will come back when you wake up. It's going to be awhile," Dr. Brown said.

"Bye, Mom. You will be fine. I'll come back and visit you later," he promised.

The doctor led her to the bedroom, gave her a sharp prick and she was asleep in minutes for an indefinite period of time.

Shirley felt like a zombie during her ten-day stay in the hospital and the feeling didn't disappear when she went home. The details of life seemed surreal and she had a fifteen, thirteen and eleven-year old whose lives had been turned upside down. Paul had tried to watch out for them, but basically they had fended for themselves. Shirley wasn't able to work so she went on sick benefits and that meant a lower income. She decided to take a course and learn about computers in the hope of getting a job through the agency. And eventually she did.

Paul came to see her a few weeks after she was home. "Mom, you are not going to like this, but I have decided to go back to Campton Crossing. Unlike you and the kids, I don't like Alberta. And what happened at the hospital was too freaky for me. I love you, but I don't ever want to go through that again. I gave my notice at work and I will be heading out after that," he informed his mother. "I don't want you to go, but I understand," she replied. Shirley had come to realize that there were aspects of the illness that few people could endure and he was only twenty.

Shirley knew Susan and David were drifting away from her by the friends they were hanging around with, but her efforts to corral them were ineffective. Her latest episode opened up a chasm between them and they no longer trusted her.

One night Susan came home late. Shirley was just about to start yelling at her when Susan burst into tears. "What's wrong, Honey? Why all the tears?" she asked. Shirley sat her down in a chair and gave her some tissue.

Red-eyed, she began the story. "A bunch of us from school went out to McFaram's Ranch in Stony Plain. We had alcohol with us," she said.

"How much alcohol did the group have?" Shirley asked.

"A lot. Way more than normal," Susan said.

"Oh great," she responded. "Go on," Shirley prodded her.

"We were all getting drunk very fast. I mean even I puked, but Anna kept puking and puking. Her skin turned bluish and she looked like she was having a seizure. Her breathing was weird too. Then she collapsed and we couldn't wake her up. The guys were laughing, but I knew something was wrong. I told them, 'She needs to get to the hospital. NOW!' Mom, I thought she was dead! I was so afraid! They put her in Mike's car and drove straight to the West End Hospital. The doctor said if we had been any later in getting her to the hospital, she could have died of alcohol poisoning," Susan said as she began to sob and sob. Shirley comforted her.

"Is Anna out of danger?" she asked her.

"Yes," she mumbled.

"Did you find her mom?" Shirley asked her.

"Yes, she's at the hospital now," Susan responded.

Shirley thought the incident would turn Susan around, but not so. She had used everything in her small arsenal of parenting skills, and she became increasingly aware that rebellion ruled in her home. Her heart was broken as she contemplated asking Susan to leave. She was smoking cigarettes and pot and drinking alcohol all supplied by her friends. Worse yet, she was defiant in front of the other children.

*Lord, I don't know what to do. It's like she's slipping away and I'm powerless to prevent it. I'll correct anything I've done wrong, but I don't know how to defeat this beast I'm up against. I'm so concerned that if I don't deal with Susan quickly, her behavior will adversely affect Samantha and David. Even then, I could be too late. Help me, Lord. What should I do?*

*Behold, I am the Lord, the God of all flesh. Is there anything too hard for me? Call to Me, and I will answer you, and show you great and mighty things, which you do not know. I am your portion, therefore hope in me. I am good to those who wait for Me, to the soul who seeks Me. It is good that you should hope and wait quietly for the salvation of your Lord.* (Jeremiah 32:37, 33:3, Lamentations 3:24-26)

The final blow came the next week. Susan stayed out over night at an unknown location. From early morning Shirley began making calls to try and locate her. By 10:30 a.m. she had an address. Just as Shirley approached the home in the north end of Edmonton, Susan came out of the house.

"Get in the car," Shirley spoke sternly.

Susan complied.

"This has got to end today," Shirley said to her. "From now on you will have an 11:00 o'clock curfew."

"No, I will not accept that. I can't say 'yes' when I know I won't keep it," Susan said calmly.

"Then where will you live? Because I have come to the end of living in your rebellion," Shirley replied calmly.

"Sandra is asking her mother and she should hear in a couple of days," she said.

"Okay, I guess that is that," Shirley said sadly. Strangely enough, Shirley felt a sense of relief at the turn of events. They drove home in silence. Susan moved out the next day, two months after Christine left. Shirley attended some of Susan's baseball games, but it was very awkward for her. She wanted to show Susan that she hadn't quit on her. It stirred up all the pain each time she went to see her play, but it was the only way to tell Susan she loved her in the situation.

At the same time, David's disruptive, bullying behavior at the Christian school continued. Eventually he was expelled. In the public school system, David befriended two more bullies and made sure he was in charge. The other two had more street smarts and David quickly adopted them. Shirley didn't like what was developing, but her attempts to curb the relationships failed. David was becoming bolder, defying her at every turn. "David, if you don't stop your rebellion, I will send you back to B.C. to your dad," she told him. Shirley wondered if he needed his father at this time more than his mother.

David was not yet thirteen, but had passed the six-foot mark. He crossed the line one more time. He came home when he decided and not the agreed upon time. "David, I don't want to lose you. I want you to know how serious I am about you obeying the rules. Tonight you will sleep in the garage. It's my last ditch attempt to have you change your behavior before I send you to your father. There are plenty of blankets to keep you warm, but I'm sure it won't be comfortable," she said.

"That's not fair. Susan got plenty of chances before you kicked her out," David retorted.

"It's because of what happened with Susan that I'm making these choices. She wore me out. I pleaded with her over and over again to do what was right. It looks like I left it too late. And now you're doing the same thing. Obey, or know that you will be living with your dad!" She explained. She handed him the sleeping gear and he went out to the cottage-sized garage.

There was no change. David continued to bully, steal with his friends, and break curfew. In exasperation, she sent him to his dad.

With only Samantha and Shirley left and a lowered income, Shirley could no longer afford the five-bedroom house. She moved to a small area in her best friend's house. Samantha moved to St. Catharines, Ontario to provide childcare for her cousin. Samantha called frequently and said the same thing each time. "Mom, I'm sure God is telling us to move to St. Catharines. Please pray about it and see what He is telling you to do," she would plead. Then she told her about all the fun she was having.

Shirley had loved Edmonton and wanted to stay, but her job came to an end. The position was funded by a grant and she had been there the full year. Some of her family was in the St. Catharines area, but she had no desire to move there. Susan moved back west to British Columbia to live with her dad because he had offered her a car, so going east to Ontario put David, Susan, and Paul at a great distance from Samantha and Shirley.

There was now no reason to stay. Shirley sold her car for half of what she had paid for it four years earlier, bought an airplane ticket and went alone to meet Samantha in Ontario. As she flew east, she reflected on the family's time in Edmonton. She had arrived with so much and was leaving with so little.

*Lord, what happened? How did I get so off course? If it weren't for your love for me, I would be drowning in a sea of guilt. I surrender my understanding to You and I trust that You can redeem my life and all its mistakes. Change my heart and teach me to love others as You do. Please, do not leave nor forsake my children, but lead them into a deep and personal relationship as You have with me. You are a great God and I love You so.*

# 9

## *Crushed, But Not Defeated*

It was a beautiful time of year for a new beginning. The frosty mornings turned to warm afternoons with sounds like firecrackers scaring the crows from the vineyards of Jordan. The leaves floated to piles on the ground, as in Shirley's childhood memories.

When Shirley arrived in St. Catharines, Ontario she had so little money that Samantha and she had to live in separate locations. Samantha lived with her cousin while Shirley stayed with her sister, and her niece and nephew arranged a job for her. Shirley bought a clunker and picked Samantha up each morning for school before going on to work at her family's company. Being with family at work and at home was a new experience for her and she felt secure in the arrangement.

Five months passed in St. Catharines before Shirley was able to acquire an apartment for Samantha and herself. They had only been in it a month when Shirley received a call from British Columbia that would usher in unexpected changes. "My name is Delores Delgado and I am calling from the Social Services Department for north Vancouver Island. There has been an incident with your husband

and your son David, and I have removed him from the home. David would like to live with you. Are you willing to have him?" she asked.

Shirley was so excited at the thought that David wanted to come back that she forgot to ask about Susan. She called Delores back and asked if Susan could come as well and Delores said she would run it by her supervisor. Delores phoned Shirley three days later with a date, time, and flight number for David and Susan. Samantha saw her mom's tears as she spotted her brother and sister approach the luggage rack at the airport. She nudged her arm and said, "It's only David and Susan." But when they were finally beside each other they all shed a few tears.

"Mom, it was awful," Susan told her later. "I was sleeping and kind of foggy when I heard David screaming, 'Don't hit me, Dad, don't!' I ran down the stairs and saw Dad beating David with a belt. I was so furious that I ran at him and yelled, 'What are you doing? You are a big man! Pick on someone your own size. You ought to be ashamed of yourself!' " Dad was too stunned to reply. Out of the corner of my eye I saw David leave the house. He was motioning me to follow, but I needed to get some more sleep. Later David told me he went to his friend's and that's how Social Services got involved."

"And then I asked if you could come too," Shirley jumped into the conversation.

"Yeah, and the counselor asked me if I wanted to live with you. Mom, I am so sorry for how I acted in Edmonton. Can we start all over again?"

The return of David and Susan was an answer to prayer. But four adult bodies in a two-bedroom apartment was a challenge! Many a family had to do it and Shirley knew she could make it work – somehow. At times they were glad that they were together again. At other times, they didn't know how to live with so little space. There were many territorial fights and they seemed to be back to where they started.

Shirley joined a small church of fifty people and one day after the service, an older lady asked her for tea that afternoon.

"Sure. Is 3:00 o'clock okay?" Shirley asked.

"That would be great. Do you have our address?" Margaret asked.

"Yes, see you then," she said.

When Shirley turned on their street, she realized she had forgotten their address. She whispered to the Holy Spirit, "Please help me. I know I should have written it down." She continued driving and then pulled the car over, not realizing she was at the right place. Margaret came out of the house where she was stopped and waved at her. *Thank You, Lord,* Shirley said.

As they were having tea in the living room with her husband Sam, Margaret explained the reason for the invitation. "Sam and I have raised a large family and we understand how important it is for children to have space. We realize you are doing the best you can and that it must be very crowded, especially since David doesn't have a bedroom. We have an unused bedroom here and we were wondering what you would think if Susan lived with us until you had more room," she said.

Shirley was overwhelmed with their generous offer and when approached, Susan agreed too and moved in shortly afterward. They had an old piano and Susan loved to create her own music. The peace of the household and Sam's fatherliness created the healing atmosphere that her heart both longed for and needed. Crying tears of gratitude, Shirley prayed, *Jesus, I have seen your hand so many times. Thank you for being a father to the fatherless.*

Nearly a year later, Margaret and Sam came to undergird them again. Shirley had regular visits with them, especially Margaret, but one day she looked her right in the eyes and Shirley knew she was about to make a very serious statement. "Shirley, Sam and I have wanted to help different single parents, but have not because of the way they have bad-mouthed their spouses, especially in front of their children. Neither of us has ever heard you do that. We have a small amount of money we want to give you for a deposit on a home. That way you can all be together," she said softly. Big, fat alligator tears rolled down Shirley's cheeks.

"I don't know what to say. Your affirmation is astounding," she said and the dam of tears was released. "I have never known such generosity. I really believe this is the way God intended us to relate to one another. I don't have to tell you how significant having our own house will be. Thank you, thank you and again thank you," she said.

Sam came with her to look at the first few homes. He taught her what she should be looking for and what she needed to avoid. "When you think you have found the house you would like to buy, call me and we can go through it together. You will do fine. Keep praying," he said as he got in his car and drove away.

Shirley found a unique little house in central St. Catharines close to bus stops and walking distance to schools. It was an old house with two bedrooms for the girls on the main floor, a huge dining/living room with hardwood floors that became a benched alcove which looked onto the main street. In the upstairs space, there was a 20' x 12' loft with an adjacent bathroom. Downstairs was not finished, but there was a semi-finished bedroom. Sam gave his approval and they moved in.

David had his man-cave downstairs and was glad to be near the TV. Susan took the opportunity to experiment with her desire to paint. Every inch of the walls and ceiling became sky and clouds. She painted the constellations of the stars just above her bed. Samantha was happy with her own space and eager to connect with her friends at Denis Morris High. Shirley felt like a queen in her huge get-a-way loft, but her ears could still hear if there was any trouble downstairs.

They had many fun times with her sister Diane and her husband Mike, their two children, spouses and four grandchildren. They met for everyone's birthday, the holidays, some anniversaries and at times spontaneously. Diane was a great cook and Shirley never had so much fun eating. Her kids were in seventh heaven as cooking and baking were not one of her strengths. After they ate, they cleared the table to play cards or a board game and the competition was on. David was awakened by the challenge, Samantha was fierce in her strategies, and Susan was content to be with her family. David was only six years older than Diane's oldest grandchild. All seven children seemed to form a sub-family apart from the adults and the hours spent with her sister and her family were very rich in healing for her and her children.

Needing to make more income with the purchase of the house, Shirley took a job at a car leasing company. After six months, she received a promotion and a raise. Susan was also able to get part-time employment there. However, in her new position she was given access to more information. When she asked her boss about some questionable practices, he asked her to work more closely with the head salesperson. She listened to Bob while he was on the phone, then she appealed to the boss.

"I have been concerned for some time by the paperwork I have seen. I just heard Bob tell a customer that we would pay for any repairs after they have possession of the car. That's not true. That is not our policy. He's like a gunslinger marking the notches on his gun," she told the boss.

"But, Shirley, he's selling more cars than anyone in Ottawa or London. He's outselling the head office in Calgary!" he said.

"At what cost? How many lied-to customers will it take before the truth about this company is exposed?" she asked him.

"You are over-reacting. People get angry and then they soon forget," he replied.

"Doesn't anyone care that our customers could end up with no car and an obligation to pay back their loan at 21% interest? How many will have to face bankruptcy possibly for a second or third time?" she asked.

"They choose to do business with us," her boss replied.

"They thought they were doing business with people they could trust. Our number one salesperson is compiling a list of dissatisfied or soon-to-be-dissatisfied customers. If head office is sanctioning this kind of practice, it won't be long before the whole company crumbles," she stated her opinion. Within the year, the office in St. Catharines, along with the other two Ontario offices closed their front doors for good. A number of months later, the head office in Calgary closed.

Susan was delighted to land a job with jet boat tours in Niagara-on-the–Lake. For the winter, she snagged a job in Whistler, B.C. as a ski guide. Both jobs came as an answer to prayer. It was the spawning of many adventure employment trips she would embrace. Shirley had mixed emotions about Susan's new found boldness. She was excited to see her blossoming confidence, but the idea of being apart from her made Shirley feel uncomfortable. Susan's absence played on her mind continually. She had nightmares about her getting hurt on the mountain. She began to obsess over her well-being. She fought to keep it under control, but could never manage to quell the struggle.

Shirley applied for a job at a company whose sole purpose was to invent and market a mechanism to reduce and/or stop the incidences of eighteen wheeler tractor trailers losing their tires on the highways, killing people and causing great personal damage.

*Lord, I have been hearing about this for years. Please give me favor to get an interview and then grace to know what to say to get the job.*

Three days later she received a call for an interview. She sat with the president and Don, the man who had called her, and fifteen minutes into the interview Shirley knew she had the job. She started the following Monday at 8:00 a.m.

She worked with seven men – from president to mechanic to scientist. Her role was receptionist, secretary, and bookkeeper. She was delighted to be where she was needed and grateful to be treated with respect. The device to prevent tires from coming off had already been created by the time she arrived, and now the company was in the marketing stage. For over a year she witnessed the frustration of the men not getting any contracts, and she began to wonder what she could do about the situation. It weighed on her mind heavily. With the stress of raising her teenagers and copious amounts of coffee (she later learned that caffeine depletes the effectiveness of lithium) her mood swung over-the-top high.

In one afternoon she gathered all the company information she could without arousing suspicion and left the office on a false pretense. She rented a car and made her way to Toronto Pearson International Airport and booked a flight to Vancouver with a layover in Edmonton. She felt like a secret agent on an urgent mission. Her girlfriend picked her up at the Edmonton airport.

"Shirley, oh my goodness!" she said as she hugged her. "Are you okay? What's going on?" she asked as she witnessed Shirley's agitation.

"My company has sent me out here to sell the device that will stop trucks from losing their tires and killing people," she said.

"How much time have they given you to do this?" she asked.

"Twenty-four hours. Then I have to meet Susan in Whistler," she replied.

Barbara laughed, but then she said, "Don't you think that is a bit unrealistic?" She saw the disappointment on Shirley's face. "C'mon, Honey, let's go home and have a bowl of soup," she said.

After they ate, they went to the living room and talked for hours. Barbara concluded with, "My friend, I don't know whether to help you get to the psych ward or take everything at face value. I've had so much fun with you tonight. I've never seen you so loose. Are you sure you are really okay?" she asked.

"I'm fine, Barbara. Maybe we should get some sleep. The plane leaves at 11:15 in the morning," she said, knowing she would not sleep that night.

The next morning, Shirley caught the flight to Vancouver and the bus to Whistler. As she stepped off the bus, she saw Susan. Shirley could tell by the look on Susan's face that she was concerned about her mother. They embraced and she asked, "You're high aren't you?"

"No, Susan. I'm not high. I was just lonely and wanted to see you," she replied.

"How long have you been high?" she persisted.

"Now, Susan, what makes you think I'm high?" she asked her.

Susan told her later that from experience, both her erratic behavior and the mother/daughter role reversal indicated that she was high and pushing the subject would only agitate Shirley. Susan had formulated a plan to get her mother to the hospital upon hearing she was arriving.

She changed the subject. "Do you have a credit card?"

"Yes, I do," she replied.

"Follow me," she said as she led her to a hotel that was close by. Susan booked a room for one night.

When they were in the room, Shirley asked her, "Why are you angry with me? I came all the way out here to see you. I haven't done anything wrong."

"I'm sorry, Mom. I've been working a lot lately and I'm a bit grouchy," she said as she stretched out on the bed. "I need some sleep and so do you. Please, Mom, go to sleep!" she said.

Shirley lay down on the bed beside her and stroked her hair. Susan was asleep in only a few minutes. Shirley wasn't tired. Very quietly, she slipped her coat on and went for a stroll in the village. When she returned, Susan was still sleeping. Shirley decided to take a bath. Susan slept through that too. Shirley was able to get twenty minutes of sleep after relaxing in the hot water. It was still in the middle of the night. She read and drew pictures until Susan awoke at eight in the morning.

"Are you hungry?" Susan asked.

Shirley nodded 'yes.'

"Let's go get something to eat. Don't say anything to anyone. Just tuck your arm into mine and let me handle the conversation. Ready?" Susan asked.

Shirley nodded again and they went out the door to the village arm in arm. Shirley wanted more freedom while she was in Whistler, but she didn't want Susan to be angry with her.

While walking through the village, Susan suggested they go shopping in Vancouver. They would catch the next bus.

"That's a great idea!" Shirley said.

While waiting for the bus they went into a convenience store to get a few snacks. Susan was looking around when she bumped into her mother in the center aisle. "Mom, what are you doing? You have four, five, six, seven chocolate bars. Now put them back. You can keep one," Susan directed her.

"Oh, three please. Please, Susan," she begged.

"One, Mom," she said firmly.

"That's not fair! Please, Susan. I want three!" she demanded.

"Fine. Three," she said to the clerk as she rolled her eyes.

Shirley sat on the window side of the bus with Susan beside her. She gazed out the window with her nose pressed against the glass as they passed through the mountains. Just south of Squamish, she felt caught up in a vision. The water rose up out of Howe Sound in biblical flood proportions. It reached the highway and slammed into the rocks above the bus moving north along the ridge that bordered the highway. She ducked in order to miss the impact. She looked back to the Sound to see a medium sized island being swallowed by an enormous wave. She was frozen with fear. She was aware that what she was seeing was not in the reality of the moment, but did not know if she was seeing a prophetic vision or the result of a mind gone mad. For years, she debated which was which and only shared it with one trusted friend.

They got off at the first stop before Vancouver city center. Susan took out her phone and started dialing. "Dad, Mom and I are at Park Royal Mall in North Vancouver. Mom is sick and I don't know where the hospital is or what I should do," Shirley heard her say. Then Susan began to cry. "Okay, okay, bye," she said as she tried to wipe her tears.

Susan dialed again and within ten minutes later, a police vehicle pulled up alongside them. Shirley grabbed Susan's arm and with voiced suspicion asked, "What is he doing here?"

"Now, Mom, stay calm. He is here to help us," she said.

"Are you Susan?" the policeman asked.

"Yes," she replied. She began to cry. "I just don't know what to do for my mom. She is manic-depressive. I don't know where the hospital is and I don't know how to get her there," she said through her tears.

"It is okay, Susan. My mother is manic-depressive too. I understand. We'll call an ambulance and they will take her to a hospital. Everything will be okay," he comforted her.

Fifteen minutes after the policeman used his radio an ambulance showed up. Susan and Shirley got in. The attendants had many questions to ask.

"That's none of your business!" Shirley yelled at one of attendants.

"Mom, they need the information for their reports. You can tell them that," she coaxed her mother.

"Divorced! I still think it is none of your business," Shirley declared.

"Mom, just answer the questions," Susan said.

Finally, they arrived at the hospital. Susan told her mom to take a seat while she approached the front desk of the emergency department. "See that lady over there? She's my mother. Her name is Shirley Peterson and she is manic-depressive. She has been on a high for at least four days and has had only a few hours of sleep in that time. Three days ago she left her job in Ontario on a pretense, stole inside company information with the grandiose idea of selling the product to someone in Alberta, told no one including her teenage son where she was going and then came to me in Whistler. I must leave in sixty minutes to catch the bus back to Whistler. If you are able to see her before then, that would be great, but I must leave regardless. Thank you for your help," Susan informed the receptionist.

Susan came and sat beside Shirley and took her hand. "Everything is going to be fine, Mom. Aunt Diane is making arrangements for you to get back to Ontario. The doctor will treat you here for a while and then you will be able to go back home. I must leave soon, so if they haven't called you by then, I'll have to go," she said.

"Do you really have to go?" Shirley asked.

"Yes, Mom, I do," she replied. "I would like to pray for you," she stated. She took her mother's hand and began, "Jesus, please surround Mom with your angels and make her stay in Vancouver a short one. Breathe healing into her life, for her mind and her body are troubled; prepare the way for her as she returns home. Thank you for your love for Mom in all situations. In Jesus name I ask. Amen," she concluded.

Thirty minutes later Shirley said goodbye to Susan and a nurse led her to the psychiatric ward. The doctor prescribed medication that left her feeling drowsy and said she could go home as soon as he thought she had stabilized. She had a great deal of time to herself and she went searching for a Bible. She found a Gideon's Bible and started flipping through the pages.

*Lord, if there is anything you want to say to me, I am up for it.* Her fingers stopped on Proverbs and she read from Proverbs 11:2. '*When pride comes, then comes shame; But with the humble is wisdom.*' She felt uncomfortable as she read those words. She jumped to her favorite book, Isaiah, and read from 2:11. *'The lofty looks of men shall be humbled, The haughtiness of men shall be bowed down, And the Lord alone shall be exalted in that day.'*

Shirley spoke out loud to God, "No, that couldn't be! Me? Pride? No way. You are not telling me I have a pride issue! That doesn't make sense. She pushed the pages along hoping to find more redeeming words. She stopped at Obadiah 1:3. *'The pride of your heart has deceived you.'* She said the words again and again and she began to cry and then sob. She did not understand what was happening, but she knew she was broken. She wasn't who she thought she was and she felt shame at the idea of having any connection with the word 'pride.'

*Jesus, Jesus, Jesus*, she cried as she grabbed a bunch of tissues. *Have I heard you correctly? Is my heart full of pride?* She sat in silence for a period of time. *My God, my God, how do I fix it? How could I fix it? I don't know how it got started. It is the worst thing I have ever found out about myself. I feel yucky and dirty. Can you fix me?* She sat still for a long time.

She was thinking of Jesus when she saw a picture in her mind's eye. To her left there was a high mountain covered with huge boulders and to her right was luscious, green grass shimmering in the wind. Jesus was standing at the foot of the mountain looking at her. He extended His right arm towards the mountain and said, *Your journey is to the top of the mountain. You cannot proceed until I have cleared the path of the boulder that opposes you. Step into the new territory and rejoice in Me as your king. Wait, I say, wait until I remove the next boulder before you proceed. Moving in your own strength will cause the full weight of the boulder to come against you.* Then He moved His left hand toward the grassy area. *Don't be deceived by the shimmering, green grass. It is the way of destruction. Put your foot on it,* he instructed me. As soon as she stepped on it, life-sucking worms awakened and began to eat her flesh! She pulled back and they disappeared. Her heart was pounding and she looked back to Jesus.

*I am the Giver of life. Wait on Me and I will lead you up the mountain. Wait on Me and I will give you the desires of your heart*, He promised and the picture in her mind faded.

Shirley felt a shiver go down her body. The truth of His words pierced her heart and emotions. She knew He was prescribing her a way of mental health as He intended it. His instructions were to go up the mountain, wait on him, and rejoice in what He had done. He warned her of the seductive dangers that led to mental illness. She had a revelation of her puffed up self-importance that ignored common sense both in this episode and ones before. His way led to health and wholeness and her way through the shimmering grasses was driven by a demand for immediate gratification. She was seduced by the desire of easily attainable glory for herself, which ultimately led to another episode of medication and confinement.

Then she heard someone calling her for supper and she whispered, "Thank you, Jesus." She walked down the corridor to the dining hall.

# 10

## *Breakthrough*

Shirley was released within two weeks. The high was over and now, feeling defeated as she flew home, she had to face the down side. The depression part of the episode was so much lower than a normal mood swing, and she was trying to fight that off. David was numbed by the frequency of episodes and the resulting abandonment. Samantha called from college in her cheery voice, but as soon as Shirley finished the conversation, she cried from the disappointment of letting herself be deceived again. She didn't want to talk to her sister about it because of the shame she felt. Shirley wasn't ready for her sister's positive, humorous upswing of what had taken place. And Shirley lost her job.

"I am so sorry, Shirley," Don said. "I have been talking to the others about your returning to work and they are really close-minded. Only one of them had any understanding. The rest are afraid. Some of them think it will affect business adversely. You are a very good woman and you did excellent work for us, but you knew these guys were an odd collection of birds. Like I said, I'm really sorry that this was the outcome. If you ever need a reference,

I will give you one. I'll tell them what a great worker you are and say nothing about this incident."

"Thanks so much, Don. I really appreciate all your help," she said and hung up. She thought about each of the guys and felt a deep sense of shame at the thought of ever meeting one of them in town. Her only available source of income now was a disability pension, but that took weeks of doctor visits and paperwork. David was helping her financially from his part time job, but he was leaving for college in less than four months. Her savings dwindled to nothing and the unpaid bills began to pile up.

Susan came home in time for her summer job. She noticed her mother's behavior changing.

"Mom, what are you doing?" Susan asked.

"What do you mean, 'What am I doing?' " Shirley asked her.

"Mom," Susan said with disgust, "you are going high," then rephrased it, "you are *choosing* to go high! Your circumstances are not the greatest, but don't choose to go off into that world of grandiose thoughts where you start thinking you are going to be prime minister. It hurts you and it hurts us. I can see that you are starting to cross that line. C'mon, Mom. We are all going to be gone this fall. You have got to learn how to take care of yourself and make healthier choices," she said. It was a simple conversation. It had profound implications. The thought that Shirley had a measure of control over her illness was both overwhelming and exhilarating. Although she could hear the truth of her daughter's words, she did not like the rebuke.

When Shirley experienced heaviness in her chest and anxiety and panic in her heart, she called her pastor.

"Bob, that thing is happening again," she cried out.

"Okay, Shirley, can you hold on for a little bit?" he asked. "Give us half an hour and then come over and Blanche and I will pray for you," he encouraged her.

Shirley paced back and forth across the living room floor. She prayed in tongues and hoped David would not come home and interrupt her. As she drove the short distance to their house, tears clouded her vision. She asked the Lord for protection.

"Shirley, do you have any idea what has brought this on?" Bob asked her as they settled into the counseling room downstairs.

"No, I just feel like I'm going to explode," she responded.

"Okay, we will ask the Holy Spirit to lead us," he directed.

Shirley started to tremble and shake, her teeth chattering uncontrollably. Blanche reached for a blanket and wrapped her in it tightly.

"Father," Bob prayed, "we want to acknowledge our need for you. You alone know the root of what Shirley is experiencing and You alone know how to lead her to freedom. We take authority over all the powers of darkness and any schemes that interfere or distract from Your plan for Shirley this day, in Jesus name. All lying spirits be silenced in Jesus name and for His sake and glory. Holy Spirit, we invite you to come and lead us into all truth in regards to Shirley's mind, will, and emotions. Breathe your healing breath on her and set her free."

She continued to shake and tremble.

"Shirley, I have a picture in my mind's eye. If it has any significance to you, that's great, but if it doesn't, we'll discard it and continue to wait on the Holy Spirit," he told her.

"Okay," she replied.

"I saw a young girl about four or five years old and she was throwing a ball up against a red brick wall. Someone from inside the house was beckoning her in, but she seemed very reluctant to go inside," Bob explained the picture.

By the time he said the words 'throwing a ball' Shirley knew she had the same picture in her mind's eye and she came unglued. She cried. She sobbed. She wailed. It seemed as though the release of pain was coming from the depths of her soul. Blanche rushed to get her more tissue and comfort her. The crying subsided after thirty minutes.

"What were you experiencing?" Bob asked gently.

"I saw Jesus in that place you described. It was the side of my house and I was that little girl. I became aware of how much Jesus loved me at that time of my life. I became upset because as a child, I did not feel loved. I don't know why I was reluctant to go into the house, but even with Jesus there I felt afraid to go inside; I didn't feel safe," she told Bob and Blanche.

"You remain resting and when you think the Holy Spirit is finished with you, come upstairs and we'll have a cup of tea," Bob said. Shirley visited their couch in the basement often for a period of two years. Many times while resting, she simply fell asleep.

Coupled with their love and help were the wonderful nights Shirley spent at a church in Toronto.

She looked for every opportunity to be there. As she gained more insight into who Jesus was, his love for her exploded from within. The message of the 'Father's Heart' broke the chains that shackled her mind. She had never considered how Father God had loved her unconditionally, as she had always confused it with her earthly father's imperfect love. And as she heard the story of the prodigal son and meditated on its meaning, she caught a picture of a father's love she had longed for, sought after, but never found.

Like the prodigal son, Shirley broke the Father's heart when she ran away from him instead of to him at her mother's death. She filled her life with all the things she thought would satisfy her – men, travel, even riches. Instead, she silently heaped offense after offense inside until her heart was like a raging volcano about to erupt, destroying herself and those around her. After years of hating God, she called to Him in desperation and He came to her in the comforting words of Psalm 23. He took her from hopelessness to hope when she realized this kind of love was real and available to her personally. Due to this revelation, worship came to life and was filled with dancing, joy, celebration, and tears.

One night the speaker diverted the meeting with, "I believe the Holy Spirit is directing us to pray for anyone suffering with mental illness. If that is you, please come down to the front. We are family. We love you and there is no shame here." As a woman about Shirley's age put a hand on her shoulder and prayed for her, she felt an infusion of peace and Shirley's body fell gently backwards. The lady came along side Shirley and continued, "Father, meet her every need. Please release the gift of intimacy. May she know you more deeply than she ever has before. Thank you, Jesus," she prayed as she held Shirley's hand. Every hint of the Holy Spirit interacting with her was like a warm healing ointment being poured over her head. It was hope, love, and joy all in one.

It was a warm day in June in the year 2003. Shirley sat soaking up the sun on her face on the back porch. "God, I have no idea where I'm going. All the kids will be gone by the fall and I really don't want to stay here in St. Catharines. I know there has been lots of good come out of being here, but I really want to live in Edmonton or out in B.C. And all these bills and the mortgage, how do they get paid? You must have a plan. I certainly don't. Jesus, Jesus, my Jesus," she said. She put her face in her hands and rested.

In her mind's eye, she saw a picture. Jesus and Shirley were sitting on a wharf dangling their feet over the water. Shirley noticed a red and white lighthouse at the end of the wharf. She recognized the surroundings as Steveston, British Columbia. There was a small fishing boat coming out of the harbor. Pete, her first husband, was on it with a few people. He waved to them and they waved back. A second vessel came along and Allen, her second husband, was on it. He waved and they waved back. The sun was shining and a warm breeze was blowing. Jesus and Shirley were laughing, although there were no words spoken. There was a wonderful peace with Him beside her.

Shirley was still on the back porch when she heard the front porch doorbell ring. A very pleasant man stood before her and said, "Hi, I'm Bill Southerly. I am the pastor of a new church here in St. Catharines and I just wanted you to know we are here. Our church is called Lighthouse Baptist and we are located on James Street." They chatted for a few minutes and she returned to her back porch.

"Okay, Lord, what is with the lighthouse?" she asked.

The next day while sorting some books at the Mental Health office, Shirley came across two books with a lighthouse on the cover. The next day, she saw a commercial for golf. It had a lighthouse in the background. Margaret and Sam picked up Susan and herself for an evening at the church in Toronto. They told Shirley and Susan of their recent trip to British Columbia. They had visited Lighthouse Park. For thirty days in a row, Shirley saw a picture, heard a story, or saw something on television or some other place with a lighthouse on it.

With the picture and the thirty days of seeing the lighthouse, Shirley was convinced that it was God's plan for her to go back to British Columbia at some point. Each of her children moved to British Columbia after their schooling, so it all made sense. She didn't know how or when that could happen in her present circumstance.

Years later, the Lord gave her friend Karen a revelation about the lighthouse. *You are the lighthouse built on a rock at the end of a piece of land. Behind the land is a harbor. A storm is raging and many boats are in the water trying to navigate the storm. Some of the boats are big and some small; some are not doing very well. All the boats are heading for the safe harbor behind the lighthouse. Its light shines brightly, but the lighthouse is also pounded by the waves.*

*You are the lighthouse set on the rock. I (Jesus) am the rock. As long as you are secure in Me, you will not be moved. You will feel the pounding of the waves, but do not fear. Your job is not to rescue the people in the boats. Your job is to keep your lamp lit and your glass clean, and shine the way to safe harbor.*

Shirley often had the TV on while she worked at home as it served as company. On July 2, 2003, she watched Jacques Rogge, President of the International Olympic Committee, as he announced the winning bid for the 2010 Olympics. She had been praying for the Vancouver/Whistler bid and felt attached to this incredible possibility. When he said the winner was Vancouver/Whistler, tears of joy fell down her face. Thousands of Canadians at GM Place and Whistler exploded into jubilation and her heart burst with patriotism she had known all her life, but found a place for that day.

Later that same day, in the quietness she approached her God. *Abba, Daddy, I want to be in Whistler for the Olympics. I want to be near my kids, but I also want this for me. It's most likely the only Olympics I will ever be near. Could you place me in a job where I could watch the Olympics come in, where I could watch them develop? You have told me to ask you for the things I need and want, so I'm asking you for this. I know that you know what's best for me and you have good plans for my life. I trust you. Thank you for loving me. Amen.*

Shirley's income was less than $600.00 per month. She took each of the bills as they came in and put them in a medium-sized basket. *This one is yours, Lord. Thanks for being my provider.* She had no idea how they would be paid. Susan was heading back to Whistler at the end of the jet boat season and would remain in B.C. Samantha was already working there. David was leaving for college in Lindsay, Ontario in only a few more weeks and then he too would move to B.C.

Shirley decided to sell the house even though she could not profit from it. She could find rent lower than her mortgage. Grant, a man from church said that he was looking for a place to buy. He came over to her house twice before they agreed it would be beneficial to both of them for him to buy the house. They drew up the papers and decided that moving day would be on August 31, 2003. Tamara, a Christian she had recently met, would rent Shirley a room. Grant had complications with the financing and they rewrote the agreement to say that he was responsible for paying the mortgage until he could officially buy the house.

The contract in place, Shirley took three house-cleaning jobs to give her some structure and have a few extra pennies. It was very humbling. But in spite of her efforts to remain healthy, she succumbed to a deep, black hole of depression. Her children were her reason for living and they were gone. If she hadn't vowed to herself that she wouldn't commit suicide, she surely would have planned for her death at this time. But she didn't want her children to experience the shame and guilt of such a choice.

Shirley slept for eighteen hours a day. She talked to the Lord occasionally, but either He didn't hear her or she didn't hear Him.

One morning while she was contemplating getting up or going back to sleep, she heard the voice of the Lord say, *Choose LIFE or choose DEATH.*

*Lord, I don't even know what life looks like right now*, she replied.

A picture came to her mind of her walking down a street.

*Yes, Lord, I could do that. I will start tomorrow. I'll set the alarm and go for a walk*, she promised. She pulled the cover over her head and went back to sleep.

The next morning the alarm went off. She pulled on her pants. She looked back at the bed and caved in. She crawled back under the covers and made herself snug and warm. Just as guilt came to envelop her, she heard, *This is the closest you have come to a walk in months. Celebrate.* She responded, *Yes, Lord. Thank You, Jesus, for the little victories*, and she relaxed and fell asleep. The next morning, she managed her pants, her socks, and her top while she sat on the side of her bed. She looked at herself and then went back to the bed. "Thank You, Jesus, for progress," she said and crawled under the covers instead of going further.

In this same manner, it took her four days to get to her bedroom door, ten days to the door of the house. Finally, on the eleventh day, she managed to get out the door and walk one block. Then she celebrated! She danced and shouted! "I did it! I did it!" she rejoiced. She was free in some way she did not understand, but surely felt. She wanted anyone who could hear her to know. The next day she walked a few blocks and the day after that a few more. Shirley was excited with her performance as long as she walked more than the day before and she would not accept less. In two weeks, she had a forty-block area of St. Catharines marked off, and she made it her absolute daily minimum, rain or shine. She began to notice new things as she walked and talked with the Lord every morning at 7:00

a.m. She was breathing in new life and the depression was falling off in layers – literally she was losing weight.

One morning during an intimate conversation with the Lord, Shirley saw herself as a four-year old in her bedroom. It was like she was watching a movie. The Holy Spirit had taken her to this scene before, but she ran away like that little girl yelling, "Not yet, not yet! I am not ready!" On this occasion, she felt ready to have a look at whatever it was the Spirit wanted to show her, but she was still afraid. "Okay, Lord, okay. I'm ready, but please go slowly." She began to cry as the details unfolded.

Her parents often had a party at their house on Saturday nights for the members of their bowling team. They came over after bowling to watch the hockey game and play cards. One night one of her parents' friends was so drunk he bounced off the stair walls all the way up to their only bathroom on the second floor where her bedroom was. When he left the bathroom, her ears listened for the direction of his footsteps. They were coming towards her bedroom and not returning downstairs. *Why was this person coming to her room?* Her heart began beating very fast. She could hear him say, "Shirley, little Shirley, are you in there? I want to see your cute little ringlets," he said.

Shirley relaxed because she knew it was Mr. Tash, their neighbor. He always made reference to her ringlets. When he came through the door, he came over and sat on the side of her bed and a strong smell came with him. He leaned over and gave her a wet kiss and her body tensed. Something was wrong and she did not understand it. She cried out for her daddy, but he did not hear her. Mr. Tash got on top of her and kept kissing her with wet slobbery kisses. She cried out again, but no one came. He molested her and then he went back down to the party. She tried to tell her parents the next morning, but her four-year old understanding had no words for this experience. They thought she was saying that Mr. Tash gave her a kiss.

Unbeknownst to Shirley, the memory of the incident was buried in the deep recesses of her mind only to surface forty-nine years later. Its rebirth, in her adult body, drew deep-seated anger and fear as she looked at her abuse. Her sobs turned to wailing and from the depths of her being she released the pain. Every cell in her body participated in the mourning. Because she knew the deep love of Jesus for herself, she felt free to feel the anger, even rage at times, towards this man and all the men in her life who had betrayed her. She mourned the failure of intimacy with each of her husbands and yet at last she had some understanding as to why that was so. She saw the connection between the anger she was feeling and the volcanic eruptions of rage she experienced in her episodes of manic depression. She realized she was encountering the core issue behind the illness. When her fury and sadness were spent, she was aware that it was her sweet Jesus who had held her through this revelation.

And Shirley knew it was time to forgive. She understood that she was in no way agreeing with what had been done to her, but that she was giving up the right to judge those who had hurt her so deeply. Her judgment, both conscious and unconscious, had held her captive all those years. She felt relieved that someone knew what had happened to her. She was broken to see how her choices had held her from the love she so desperately needed. She asked her heavenly father for forgiveness and in light of His forgiveness for her, she forgave the man who had hurt her so deeply. The power of her childhood trauma was broken and she was ready to embrace health and wholeness.

Before this revelation, she would never have thought that Jesus would lead her to such a scary place. But now she surely knew she could trust him. Something shifted in the core of her being, and a stronger, deeper faith in Him was established.

Over nine months had passed and Grant still had not come up with the finances to buy her house. She met with him and gave him a deadline. If he couldn't come up with the money, he would have to leave the house and she would put it on the market. His tone of voice told her she was in for a battle. The deadline came and went and all his sources failed. He wouldn't leave her house, nor would he give access to potential buyers. In the next four weeks she found only misinformation about getting him out of the house. She was finally left with one option – take him to court.

After the deadline, Grant found a source of money. He had a contract of purchase and sale drawn up and began to harass Shirley to sign. One day he discovered where she parked when she was at work, and as she walked towards her car, he started his engine and drove directly at her. One wheel drove up on the sidewalk as he pulled alongside her. "You'd better sign those papers. I know you tricked my friend not to give me the money before the deadline. *Sign those papers!*" he yelled at her. Shirley turned and walked away.

Three days later, Grant and his friend came into Shirley's workplace, an information center where she was on the front desk. As soon as she saw them, she turned to her co-worker and said, "Could you please call security? I believe we have a problem."

Grant charged her desk. "Sign these papers if you know what is good for you," he threatened.

"Yes, Sir, I will get my boss," she replied and left to go to her boss' office. Her boss returned with her, but they were gone.

"What was that all about?" one of her co-workers asked.

"Well, I think he suffers from a mental illness. He sounded a bit delusional," Shirley replied.

Susan called and asked her mom if she wanted to go to the 'One Heart Gathering' July 2005 in Quebec City. Shirley thought it was a great idea and they made plans to go. Susan flew from Vancouver to Montreal and Shirley picked her up there. Together, they drove to Quebec City and were blessed to find a large apartment overlooking the river in the Old City. Conferences were always special for her because she was away from the business of life and engulfed in her relationship with Jesus.

The 'One Heart' conference was a wonderful expression of reconciliation between the French and English in Canada; the Inuit, First Nations and the Metis, all aboriginal people groups in Canada; and then all of them with the rest of the body of Christ. Four thousand believers confessed their love and commitment to God and to each other!

Shirley had had a relationship with a younger Christian man for some time prior to the conference, but she had been dishonest with him and herself. She knew she would never marry him, and she should have broken it off, but she clung to the wonderful way he treated her. At this conference, the Lord revealed to her that she needed to make a choice between her relationship with this man and her inheritance in Christ. She wanted both. It was scary for her to realize that she had the freedom of choice and had to accept the weight of consequences.

She broke it off, but the sorrow she experienced over the loss of that relationship ran deeper than she had imagined. She had left some valuables at Sally's, the home of her young man's mother. Shirley had come to love her dearly, and she knew Sally would be hurt. When she went to retrieve them, his mother said, "You sure get some strange ideas in that head of yours. You hurt my son and I will never forgive you for that."

"I'm sorry that I have hurt you, Sally. I don't expect you to understand," Shirley replied.

"What is the matter with you? Is *Jesus* going to be your husband?" she asked mockingly.

"Yes, He is, Sally," Shirley replied softly.

"And is *He* going to be your provider?" she asked.

"Yes, He is, Sally," Shirley replied softly again.

Sally allowed her to hug her and Shirley left.

After a year in the courts with Grant, there was still no resolve. Shirley wanted to see Susan for Christmas and decided to use the last of her credit. She wanted to see Whistler and dream about where she was going; despite all the uncertainty, she remained convinced that was her destination.

Susan and Shirley had lots of fun with all the activities in Whistler prior to Christmas while Susan worked at her job. By December 26th though, Susan was exhausted.

"Susan, I believe the Lord wants us to pray," Shirley told her.

"Mom, I don't have the strength. I have to have a nap first," she answered.

"Okay, I'll go for a stroll in the village and we'll pray after you wake up."

Shirley's stroll took her to the base of Whistler Mountain. Due to a lack of snow, the staff had to build a runway of snowy-ice on the bottom part of the mountain so that skiers and snowboarders could exit and go back up the lifts. The scene before her was out of order, and she contemplated what it would look like with snow everywhere.

A thought passed through her mind. *Lord, are you asking us to pray for snow?*

Shirley turned and began to walk towards the lower part of the village when she heard the Holy Spirit say, *Turn right.* She obeyed. *Turn left.* She heard His voice again. In this manner, she made many turns until she stood in front of the Conference Center. Memories flooded her mind of associations with this building. Shame. Disgrace. Rejection. This was the building she had been thrown out of, stripped of membership, excluded from the events of the Christian Conference for Canada, and cursed to hell.

In the stillness of her heart, she heard the words of Isaiah 62:2b-4, "*You shall be called a new name, which the mouth of the Lord will name. You shall also be a crown of glory in the hand of the Lord, and a royal diadem in the hand of your God. You shall no longer be termed 'Forsaken' nor shall your land any more be termed 'Desolate'. But you shall be called Hephzibah, and your land called 'Beulah'. For the Lord delights in you, and your land shall be married.* She knew the words but, in this context they touched her deeply. Tears flowed down her cheeks as she contemplated how much God loved her. She had the revelation that she would one day work in this building. She would return to Ontario and pray for her God-given place there.

Susan was waking up as Shirley came through the door. She still looked a little groggy.

"Guess what I think God wants us to pray for?" she asked.

"What?" she yawned.

"Snow!!!!!!" she shouted.

"I hope this will be a quiet request," Susan replied.

Susan disappeared into the prayer room, established before Shirley's arrival, where other requests had been made accompanied with words written on construction paper and hung with yarn from the framework of the bunk bed above. Shirley was so excited after what happened in the village that she was ready to do a 'snow dance,' but decided to slow it down to a pace Susan was comfortable with. After a few minutes, she heard a noise from the prayer room and she went in. Susan had construction paper and scissors in her hands. "What are you doing?" her mother asked.

"I'm making snowflakes, putting a scripture on them, and hanging them up there," she said.

They giggled and laughed together as they made their snowflakes and followed her pattern, suspending them from the frame of the top bunk.

Susan had a room ready for her to rent whenever Shirley was free of Ontario. They hoped it wouldn't be long before she was back. She returned to St. Catharines two days after Christmas. Susan called her January 5th. "Mom, it has been snowing since you left," she said. The answer to their quiet prayers was extraordinary. Snow records for 2005 were: November 115 cm (45 in.); December 139 cm (55 in.); January 2006 recorded 469 cm (185 in.) at Whistler/Blackcomb Mountains!

The next day, January 6th, Grant unexpectedly gave up his hold on the house. He moved out January 10th. Shirley gathered a group of good friends to repair the house and freshen it with paint. One week later after getting the house back, she put a 'For Sale' sign in the front window. Viewing was two days later. The first family who walked through the house made a full-priced offer. It was finally over. All who helped her rejoiced at the goodness of God and the fact that she was finally free!

Shirley made enough profit from the house to pay off all her debt, all lingering bills, pay her way back to Whistler, buy a computer, and be able to live for a few months until she got a job. She was even able to take a step toward her dream of writing about the reality of God in her life, and to that end, she attended a Writer's Conference in Whistler, which began in February of 2006. Her God had severed the tie from the man who was badgering her, delivered her from her debt, physically located her close to all four of her children, and put her in a position to receive the job she had asked for three years earlier.

# 11

## *Special Times*

The Whistler Writer's Conference surrounded Shirley with professional and amateur writers alike, and she was fascinated by the writing world – a brand new territory for her to discover. She gathered so much new information that she was overloaded by the afternoon of the first day. Shirley learned that there was a local writer's group that met monthly – a wonderful place to observe and to grow. She attended the meetings regularly, relishing the passion these writers exhibited. She had only one book she wanted to write while they talked about books, poetry and articles they were working on. Because of her subject, she was beginning to feel like an oddball. During this time, the Lord led her to a scripture, *Write the vision and make it plain on tablets, that he may run who reads it, for the vision is yet for an appointed time; but, at the end it will speak, and it will not lie. Though it tarries, wait for it; Because it will surely come, it will not tarry.* (Habakkuk 2: 2,3)

"Okay, Lord. I don't get it all. But I get some of what you are saying. Writing this book is not for now, but for the future. Right now, though, I really need to find work. It has been four months since I left Ontario and I am running out of money. Could you please show me where and how to find a job?" Shirley asked.

Every Thursday, a local newspaper published the latest postings for employment positions for all of Whistler. The local tourism company had a listing for a finance position. She could scarcely believe it as it was exactly what she had asked for when she was back in Ontario. It was a company from which she would surely be able to watch the Olympics develop between 2006 and 2010. Those who knew her and some who knew about her story said things like, "This is your job for sure," or "God has hand-picked this job for you," or "It's already in the bag," or "No worries, it's yours." She was sure it was her job for the taking. She applied, had an interview, and did not get the job. She was disappointed and embarrassed, but she didn't have time to feel sorry for herself because she still did not have a job.

Shirley applied for a supervisor's position in a cleaning company and got it in two days. It was exhausting, strenuous work, every day. Carrying bags of laundry, cleaning equipment and supplies up and down many flights of stairs was the norm. She had a team of three young women, each from a different country. Two of them spoke little English, which meant she had to show them what she wanted done instead of telling them. The housing units were scattered across the mountains and the valley areas of the Whistler and Blackcomb Mountains.

One day while she was driving the van down the steep, winding mountain road, reality flashed before her. To herself she said, *Okay, Lord. This is not going to work.* She envisioned herself driving down this same road in the snowy, icy conditions of winter. *No, Lord. I won't make it through this. I do not want to drive this road in the winter.* She quit at the end of the month and within a week, she had another job. She was a nanny for two families. She worked mornings at one and afternoons at the other. Both mothers allowed her any flexibility she needed. The children were delightful, and both families lived in Whistler mansions, where she cleaned and did some cooking when needed. But in January 2007 one family hired a live-in nanny from Jamaica, so that left her with only one-part time work.

During the time she held this job, her doctor advised her to see the psychiatrist who visited occasionally in Whistler. Dr. Thomasbeck and Shirley had some very candid discussions. "This is what I believe about manic depression or bi-polar disorder as it is now called," Shirley began. "I believe that bi-polar disorder does not start in the brain, but in the heart – not the physical heart, but the emotional heart – where we experience joy, sorrow, raging, peace, discord, fear, willingness to trust, and the rising up of pride in the bad sense. I believe if we get stuck on the negative emotions due to intensity or frequency of incidences, brain chemistry is affected and we are in danger of a chemical imbalance. If nothing is rectified, the symptoms of bi-polar disorder manifest themselves. Medications medicate, but they don't address the roots of the illness. For example, a woman mourns her mother's death for ten years as if the event happened last week. Her life becomes tied down by one main incident and she begins making decisions out of a framework of death, mourning, and hopelessness. From the outside we recognize this is an unhealthy response, but how is that sustained state of mourning along with day-to-day stresses affecting the chemistry of her brain? As the brain chemistry becomes unbalanced, I believe it is only a matter of time before it manifests as the symptoms of bi-polar disorder or other mental illnesses.

"That is remarkable. This is similar to our findings in our research at UBC (University of British Columbia). When is the last time you were hospitalized?" he asked.

"Over seven years ago," she replied.

"Are you still on medication?"

"Yes, lithium," she said.

"Have you ever thought of coming off it?" he asked.

"Yes, many times, but I was afraid I would have another episode if I did it too quickly. I don't know at what rate to do it," she said.

"I honestly don't know the correct rate either because there is no history of this type of action, but I can help you with that if you want to get off it. We could go slowly so that your body has time to adjust at each level," he commented.

Shirley started to lessen the amount from 1200 mg to 900 mg per day. Dr. Thomasbeck called Shirley about two weeks into the withdrawal plan asking her to delay dropping to 600 mg for six weeks. She complied. She continued being nanny for the one family. One day she did not turn up for work. She decided to talk to all the tourists at the base of Whistler Mountain. She treated everyone like they were best buddies. She had it in her head that she was going to go to the top of Whistler Mountain and go straight down as fast as she could. (Shirley didn't ski.) She challenged anyone who would listen to join her.

Shirley had no memory how she got to her doctor's office. Her doctor was making attempts to quiet her. The doctor arranged for an ambulance to come to the back door of the clinic so no one would see Shirley in this state. For Shirley, everything was a party. She enjoyed all the attention. She talked non-stop with the attendant in the back of the ambulance all the way to the hospital in North Vancouver. The facility was stark, huge, and clean; she was the only patient in a four-bed room. She was not forced down from the high with drugs. The staff were monitoring her, but allowing her to come down on her own.

Paul lived around the corner from the hospital at the time and came to visit her the next day. They had a pep talk and Shirley asked him, "Could you bring me some chocolate bars?"

"How many do you want?" he asked.

"As many as you have money for," she replied.

"Mom, I make pretty good money. I could buy a lot of chocolate bars. You will have to give me a number," he said.

Shirley thought a minute. "Okay, then twenty. Bring me twenty," she directed him.

"That's a bunch of chocolate bars!"

"Well, that's what I want and if you are the good son I believe you are, you will get them," she manipulated him.

"Okay, Mom," he laughed. "I'll get them for you."

Samantha and her husband Ted were preparing to come and see her in the hospital.

"You seem almost afraid when I mention visiting your mom," he pointed out to her.

"Oh yeah, well you haven't seen her in a manic episode," she warned.

"Don't worry, it will be fine. She always listens to me. We have a pretty strong relationship," he said to his wife.

"I won't be getting my hopes up anytime soon," she replied.

"It will be fine, Honey," he said, pulling her into his arms to comfort her.

They came to the hospital the following night. After an initial hug and greetings, Samantha spied four chocolate bars on her bureau.

"What are you doing with those chocolate bars?" she asked.

"I was craving chocolate and Paul got these when I asked for them," she replied.

"You are craving caffeine to maintain the high. Why would you do this to yourself? You need to come off your high to get well. Mom! I am so angry with you. You have learned this before. Why are you going backwards?" she asked.

"Is Mom not to have caffeine?" Ted asked Samantha.

"The doctor in St.Catharines told her "no caffeine." I don't know, maybe sugar is the problem. But she is not to have chocolate bars and she knows it," Samantha said angrily.

Paul walked in shortly after. "What were you thinking giving Mom those chocolate bars?" Samantha asked.

"What do you mean? I was just giving her what she asked for," he defended himself.

"Mom doesn't need chocolate bars," she repeated.

"Fine," Paul said and he left the room.

Ted attempted to soften the conversation. "Mom, how are you doing?" he asked.

"Not very well. It isn't very much fun in here," she said as she began to cry. "The food is rubbery and people walk up and down the hall making funny sounds in the middle of the night. Chocolate bars are my only good food. I got this disease and I keep ending up in the hospital. It's not fair. I haven't done anything wrong. I'm a good person. I really am. It's not fair," Shirley cried.

Ted walked closer to the bed and took her hand, "Mom, look at me. Look me in the eyes. You are feeling sorry for yourself and that is not going to do you any good. We love you and we want to support you in making healthy choices for yourself. We don't want to reinforce any choices that might work against you – like the chocolate bars," he said.

"Now, Mom, do you have any more chocolate bars hidden some place?" Samantha asked.

"Yes," she said as she sadly pointed to the drawer. Samantha took out another eleven bars.

"Mom, Mom, Mom," she said with disappointment. "Now is this it?" she asked.

"Yes," she said.

Paul returned to the room "Sorry, guys. I only thought I was helping Mom, not hurting her," he commented.

"It is okay, Paul. She can be pretty sneaky," Samantha said to him. "We love you, Mom," she said as she turned to Shirley. "You will get through this. You are a strong woman, but no more chocolate bars!" she teased.

Shirley remained in the hospital another two weeks before returning home. Angela, who had been her roommate for over a year, had suffered with depression. She provided insight to Shirley as she stabilized in the transition period of this episode. She knew when to be firm and when to let her find her way out of the darkness, as Angela had done years before.

"If you have been well all these years, why do you think you had another episode?" Angela asked.

"Because of my pride. It was my stupid, foolish pride. I wanted to tell everyone I was miraculously cured. As though I had some extraordinary favor with God. I wanted to be declared normal!" she said. "And sure, maybe there is an amount of time to withdraw from lithium without dire consequences, but I won't be doing that again. One unnecessary episode is enough," she finished.

Shirley lost her job as a nanny and had no income. She began a new job search as soon as she thought she was settled. Almost three months from the day she went into the hospital, she saw the posting for that same job at the local tourism company. Her first thoughts were, "Am I stable enough for such a job? Can I get past the scrutiny of an interview?"

The answer to those questions was 'no,' but she pushed through. The young man who came to interview Shirley was about the age of Paul. He briefly mentioned the details on her resume and they spent most of the time talking about the small town on Vancouver Island where Shirley had lived, a place both were familiar with. She was thankful for the diversion. He described the accounting department. It sounded like it was above her experience, but she was not going to let this opportunity pass. She found out later that it was his first time interviewing. She was sure that there was a connection between that and the fact that she got the job.

An accountant, a seasoned accounts receivable clerk, and Shirley as the accounts payable clerk all answered to the controller, the man who interviewed her. Together with the Finance Manager, they formed the accounting department in the local tourism company from August of 2007 until the summer of 2010. There were numerous meetings to keep staff abreast of new developments for the Olympics. For Shirley's position, very little would change, but the anticipation and thrill of the coming event was extremely gratifying in light of her request made back in Ontario. It was an exciting time for her; she was living her dream and she knew it.

In the midst of all the excitement, they had a family crisis. Paul had secured a job with a company working on the Sea to Sky highway from Vancouver to Whistler. They paid more money than Paul had ever earned. He started with using marijuana and later cocaine. Not knowing this, Shirley went to visit him and arrived early. The landlord recognized her and offered to let her into Paul's apartment. She had been down to North Vancouver to see Paul four months previously and his apartment was in normal bachelor shape. In contrast, the day the landlord let her in, it looked like a war zone. There wasn't an inch that wasn't covered in some kind of filth. Even the floors and walls were spattered with food or grime or some other dirty substance. She didn't want to sit down for fear something would come crawling out at her. *I don't know what this is, Lord. I have never seen this enemy. What is it, Dad?* From the still quiet voice, she heard, *Cocaine. Cocaine*, she repeated. *It must be very evil to produce death like this.*

Shortly after, she heard a noise coming from the back bedroom so she went to the door. Paul was climbing in the bedroom window.

"Hi, Mom, I wasn't expecting you so soon. How was your trip? As Paul came towards her, she asked him, "Paul, are you on cocaine?"

"How do you find these things out?" he asked. Paul was referring to the fact that over the years the Holy Spirit had given her otherwise hidden information about all her children. Paul never ceased to be amazed.

They talked all through the evening, but Paul wasn't much for talking about cocaine or why he was using it. Before they went to bed, she tried to make it as clear as possible for him. "Son, you are on a horrible path of destruction with cocaine as your friend. If you don't turn around and go the other way, you will lose your job, your apartment and be out on the street. Please make the right choice while there is still time. I love you. Good night," she said. He was gone when she awoke in the morning.

Within six weeks, Paul had lost his job, been thrown out of his apartment, and was living on the downtown eastside of Vancouver with all the other homeless people. One of the few people he kept in contact with was Samantha's father-in-law, Ken, who had befriended him years earlier.

Months after Paul had been living on the streets, Susan drove to Vancouver from Whistler on personal business. Ken and Paul had agreed to meet for coffee in Vancouver that same day. After a long talk, Ken recommended that Paul go to Whistler and be with his family, to which Paul agreed. Ken called Susan and sure enough, she was not far away. She went to the coffee shop, and after a brief discussion Susan took Paul with her and brought him to Whistler on her return. He stayed on the couch where Susan lived and four days later, he found a room. Within two days, he found two-part time jobs and started to settle in to a routine.

In June of 2009, two other women and Shirley started meeting to pray for the Olympics before work each morning. In the summer they had the light, but in the winter it was pitch black at 6:30 a.m. Occasionally they would see the light of the rising sun. Many times they would meet a local pastor who had been out praying since February 2009. They would join together for a while, and then go their separate ways.

On July 2, 2009 Shirley and her friend Elizabeth went up to the top of Blackcomb Mountain. That meant two open chairlifts to Rendezvous Restaurant, a bus ride across the mountain, and up another chairlift at Seventh Heaven to Horstman Hut at the top. Glacier skiing was the only skiing available at the time although they weren't there to ski. They went there to pray for the Olympics. They were praying while skiers were swooshing beside them. Just as they finished, a strong wind came up the side of the mountain. As they loaded on the chairlift, the wind pushed the chair hard to the right and to the left. As they moved toward the tower, the lift stopped and the chair swung wildly way up and then way down. What a thriller! They laughed, shouted, were scared, and could hardly wait to get down on solid ground. But they still had a long way to go – two more chairlifts with wind that rocked them and many stoppages all the way.

On the first chairlift, they were praying out of fright. But as they descended on the lower two chairlifts, with the village in sight they prayed proclamations of blessing over Whistler and the Olympics. Shirley was amazed and encouraged as she saw many Christian groups come into the village to walk and pray just as they had. She was informed that there were some Canadian Christian leaders who were planning to meet on an island in the Howe Sound during the days of the Olympics for the sole purpose of praying. Shirley was glad to be part of a larger prayer team.

In the lead up to the Olympics, procedures were practiced over and over again. By January 2010 security tents were in place and systems were being followed; the Armed Forces were settled in outside Whistler; extended bus routes were prepared; huge rock Inuksuks were in place welcoming visitors at the entrance to the village and at the top of Whistler Mountain; flags of many countries flew in various spots around Whistler. It was time for the celebrations to begin.

Before the gates to the athletes' village were closed, Elizabeth and Shirley went there to pray for the athletes. Never could they have imagined the horrible death of Nodar Kumaritashvili, the Georgian luge competitor. They had watched luge, bobsled, and skeleton competitions at the site the winter before. Most looked very dangerous, but she knew of no one who thought death would be an outcome. They were all devastated as they thought about the loss for his family so far away, and for the Whistler community itself. A book in which people could express their condolences to Nodar's family was established as a memorial outside a local brew-house. There was little time to mourn as they were in the beginning of the Olympics and there were many full days of activities and work ahead.

Shirley remembered listening to CBC radio in Germany in 1972 when Paul Henderson scored the winning goal in hockey over Russia.

It was a proud Canadian moment. But when Shirley watched TV as Alexandre Bilodeau came down the course during the mogul skiing event to get the gold medal, she was beside herself with excitement. Tessa Virtue and Scott Moir skated with a fairy-tale-like quality to win their gold medal. And her heart always came back to her favorite sport, hockey. Sidney Crosby brought the house down when he scored in overtime to win the gold medal against the U.S.A. for the men's hockey team. It was the best Olympics she had ever seen! And she was a part of it!

Susan had moved to Squamish, a forty-five-minute drive south from Whistler prior to the Olympics. Immediately after, Shirley went to visit her. They sat out on a hand-hewn log overlooking Howe Sound and talked about all the details of the Games and the fun they had had.

Shirley sat contemplating the street ahead while waiting for the return bus. *Father, I know it's time to leave Whistler, but I don't know where you want me to live. Each time I think of a place, I begin to think of many reasons why that would not work. I want to be where you want me to be.* Quietly, the revelation came. *Squamish? Lord, Susan will say I'm following her again!* And Shirley laughed.

She began to look for a place in Squamish. Her plan was to find work there and leave her job in Whistler. One day at the end of May she was called into the office with her three bosses. They assured her that it was not performance, but they had to start cutting back now that the Olympics were over. She could stay until the end of August 2010 at which time she would be laid off. It was perfect for Shirley. She didn't have to rush about the details in Squamish and was free to explore all her options.

*As always, you have taken care of all the details. Thank you for fulfilling my dream to come to Whistler and be part of the Olympics. And thank you for preparing the way in Squamish. You are such an awesome God. What adventure do you have for me there? Is it time for me to teach others what I have learned at your hand? Am I ready, Lord?* Shirley asked.

*Sing, O daughter of Zion! Shout, O Israel! Be glad and rejoice with all your heart, O daughter of Jerusalem! The Lord has taken away your judgments. He has cast out your enemy. The King of Israel, the Lord, is in your midst; You shall see disaster no more. In that day it shall be said to Jerusalem: Do not fear; Zion, let not your hands be weak. The Lord your God in your midst, the Mighty One, will save; He will rejoice over you with gladness, He will quiet you in His love, He will rejoice over you with singing.* (Zephaniah 3:14-17)

Jesus knew where to find Shirley when she was ready. He had His eyes on her all her life. He found her in the dried, cracked earth of the desert very close to death. He breathed on her and gave her new life. He taught her to take responsibility for her thought life and the choices she was making in an atmosphere of an intimate relationship of love, acceptance, and encouragement. Shirley is not unique. She accepted the gift of relationship with Him. He offers that same gift to every individual; He invites you to come out of your desert to wholeness, healing, and life with Him.

# *Author's Note*

In the writing of this book, my desire was to share the significance of Jesus' love in every area of life and specifically how it affected my recovery. I also wanted to provide some details of what it looks like as an individual with a seemingly healthy mind who then breaks down to a malfunctioning stage of a manic episode. I have shared how devastating the illness can be to the family and told my story publicly as well as walked beside individuals in their journey of recovery. Inquiries? You may reach me at aroseinthedesert65@gmail.com

Shirley Kennedy

CPSIA information can be obtained
at www.ICGtesting.com
Printed in the USA
LVOW12s0518270416
485522LV00001B/71/P

9 781512 733204